The Isles of the Blest

The Isles of the Blest

Morgan Llywelyn

OLMSTEAD
PRESS

An [e-reads] Book

Published in 2001 by Olmstead Press: Chicago, Illinois
e-reads: New York, New York

First published in 1989 by Ace Books: New York, New York

Cover designed by Hope Forstenzer

Text designed and typeset by
Syllables, Hartwick, New York, USA

Printed and bound in Toronto, Ontario, Canada by
Webcom Inc.

Library of Congress Card Number: 2001086657
ISBN: 1-58754-113-0

Editorial Sales Rights and Permission Inquiries should be addressed to:
Olmstead Press, 22 Broad Street, Suite 34, Milford, CT 06460
Email: Editor@lpcgroup.com

Manufactured in Canada
1 3 5 7 9 10 8 6 4 2

Substantial discounts on bulk quantities of Olmstead Press books are avail-
able to corporations, professional associations and other organizations. If you
are in the USA or Canada, contact LPC Group, Attn: Special Sales Department,
1-800-626-4330, fax 1-800-334-3892, or email: sales@lpcgroup.com.

One

BELOW THE HILL of Usna, the plain spread out like a multicolored mantle in every shade of green and gold. Ponds formed in hollows, and brooks meandered happily between fields serenaded by lark and wren and linnet.

Such a land should have been prosperous. Sometimes it was. Sometimes it was not.

Conn of the Hundred Battles stood on his hill and glared at his land. Unfair, he thought, that something so lovely should be so barren. Yet for the past two summers his cattle had not fattened sufficiently on all that green grass. Plowmen had broken the earth and sown their crops as they had done for generations, but the grain when it grew was spindly and gave a poor harvest. Sometimes it did not sprout at all.

Bakehouses stood unused much of the time for lack of grain to grind into meal. The women who should have been busy at the stone ovens were occupying their time by criticizing their menfolk. The menfolk passed the criticism along to their leader, that being one of the reasons for having a leader.

Conn of the Hundred Battles was growing tired of having everyone complain to him.

He had sent for his chief druid, Coran, and asked the priest to read the signs for him. Coran was tall and lean, with a mane of streaky gray hair that flared out from his skull even when there was no wind. From the eyes down he had the face of a fox, sharp-nosed, narrow of jaw, but his eyes were so mild the vulpine effect was quite negated. Looking at Coran you could never mistake him for anything but a druid.

Conn of the Hundred Battles matched his own name. Seen at a distance, in silhouette, he appeared square. Shoulders and chest were so broad, powerful torso built so close to the ground on wide-planted legs, that it was almost impossible to knock the man down. But when he swung a sword damage was always done. Conn had once been ruddy, but now all the redness remaining to him was in his face. His hair had gone gray like Coran's, resembling the snow-frosted pelt of an aging fox. Great bushy eyebrows guarded the high bridge of his nose, and the eyes beneath those brows were never still.

Conn had not only been in a hundred battles, he had won a hundred battles. He held this land for his tribe through his own fearsome reputation. But he might not hold it much longer if something was not done about the diminished prosperity of his people, for they were perfectly capable of choosing a new king if their current one failed them.

"Coran, what is wrong with the land?" Conn had asked the druid.

"She is tired," came the answer. Coran had thrown the sticks of prophecy into the air many times, carefully observing the patterns they made as they fell. He had gone out into the meadows and chewed thoughtfully on various grasses, reading the message sent up from the earth. He had lain flat on the ground and pressed his nose into the dirt so he could smell its health. All led to one inescapable conclusion. "The earth is a woman and she gets tired. Your men have plowed her too many times. Your cattle are so numerous they have all but cleared her of grass and she has worn herself out trying to replenish it, only to be stripped again."

Conn scowled. "Then you must do something! Perform a fertility ritual—something."

"We did that last season," Coran reminded him. "And this season is worse."

"Your magic is failing you," Conn growled. "Are you too old, druid? Usually your kind gets better with age, but if the fault is in you, I will find another druid with more power."

"I am not failing," Coran informed his chieftain haughtily, drawing himself up to his full height so he could look down his nose at the warrior. "I can do everything I always could. A fortnight ago I made sour milk turn back to sweet. I erected an unseen barrier around Fionn's house to keep his daughters in and their suitors out, until the girls get a little older. Or a little less provocative. One is much more likely to happen than the other," the druid added, remembering the plump and giggling assortment of man-hungry girls in Fionn's house.

"If you can't improve the harvest and enrich the pastures, then I don't see what good you are to me," Conn warned.

"Priests can't do everything! If we could, there would be no need for you, would there?"

Conn grinned and slapped his thigh. "Truth from the mouth of the druid. Indeed, I am needed. If you cannot solve the problem with rituals and spells, then it falls into the category of things I know how to fix. I am a warlord, son of generations of warlords. If our land fails us, I simply attack someone with richer territory and take his."

"So it has always been," Coran agreed. "But you have already taken all the land as far as we can see. If you cross your borders into new territory, you will have to move the entire tribe a considerable distance, which means new houses to build, a new fort for yourself, a general upheaval for everyone. We've been here a long time, Conn—for generations. People have sunk their roots deep into the earth . . ."

". . . the unproductive earth," Conn grumbled.

"Deep into the earth and they will not be happy about moving. You will be blamed for their discomfort."

Conn put his two fists on his hips and shook his head as a bull does when a bee keeps stinging it. "You are not giving me any answers I can accept, druid."

Coran shrugged. "For some things there are no easy answers."

"What will happen, then? At least you can tell me that much. You can still prophesy, can't you?"

"I can. And I tell you your cattle will grow thinner until some starve and die, and they will not have calves in the spring until there are no more of them than the grass can support again."

"And what of the fields, the grain?"

Gazing into a future only he could see, Coran said softly, "The earth is a goddess with power beyond ours. She will rest herself whether you will it or not."

Conn had fought and won a hundred battles, but now he felt himself caught in a trap no sword could hew open. If something was not done, he would lose the leadership of his tribe.

Sleepless and bad-tempered, he had been pacing the precincts of his stronghold for days, gazing out at the land and muttering. His wives—and he was a powerful warlord capable of clothing and feeding four wives—

took to avoiding him. The senior wife, who had in her time given permission for him to marry the second wife in order to have someone to share her work, found the best way to avoid Conn was to go to bed and stay there.

The second wife had given permission for a third wife, so fortunately she did not have to wait on her senior but could pass the chore down the line. In time it reached the fourth and newest wife, a pretty black-haired girl who looked all around but could see no one lower in the hierarchy than herself. So she carried pots and basins and ewers; she fluffed feather beds and patiently endured the invalid's complaints; and she cursed a land which had grown so poor its ruler could not afford a fifth wife.

Conn's children were no happier. The atmosphere in the fort depressed them. They took to spending more and more of their time outside their father's big round house with its thatched roof, and outside the sturdy timber palisade that protected it. They played the games that children play with balls and sticks, they ran footraces, they amused themselves in a hundred ways, and they left the real worrying to the adults. But they were all aware of something hanging over them.

So on this bright morning as Conn of the Hundred Battles stood on his hilltop and glared at his fields, he was alone, avoided like a man who has developed a loathsome disease.

"Father."

Conn spun around. His oldest son was coming up the hill with a smile on his face. Even a man in a very bad mood would have smiled in automatic response to that radiant expression, for the son of Hundred Battles was splendid to behold.

Connla, as the youth was called, was tall and lean and limber. Fiery Hair was his nickname, and well deserved, for his hair flamed in sunlight or shadow. Above cloud-gray eyes his eyebrows slanted like red-gold wings, and the perfect symmetry of his face was as yet unscarred by sword or spear.

He resembles me when I was a boy, the old chieftain thought for a moment, then remembered in honesty that he had never been beautiful. Conn was strong, but Connla had the elegance that strength can produce when mated with grace.

"Don't come up on me like that when I have a weapon in my hand, lad," the father called out. "I could have thrown this spear right through you."

Connla laughed. "You always have a weapon in your hand. If I waited until you did not, I would be in my tomb of old age."

They stood together on the hilltop. Their clothing was similar, for they both wore knee-length tunics and had cloaks fastened about their shoulders with heavy gold brooches. But Conn, as a chieftain, also wore a massive golden gorget around his neck, and his arms clanked with rings of precious metal—gold and silver and bronze. He liked to wear his wealth. It was safer on his person than anywhere else.

Young Connla had simpler tastes. His nobility entitled him to wear almost as much ornamentation as his father, but his only vanity was the care he lavished on his shining hair. He liked to feel light and free. The linen of his tunic was of sheerer weight than that of his father's, and instead of a cloak lined with wolf fur, Connla wore an unlined cloak that billowed slightly in the breeze. He glowed with youth and health. Even the whites of his eyes had the improbable blue-white luster that connotes perfect condition.

The land spread out before him was unfortunately not as healthy.

Conn of the Hundred Battles turned away from his perfect son and resumed his morose survey of his territory.

"What a grand day this is," exclaimed Connla, throwing his arms wide. "It makes me glad to be alive."

His father rolled an eye toward him. "That shows how little you know."

"What do you mean?"

"I mean you don't understand the true situation. It's easy enough to be happy when there's always meat on the spit and bread in the ovens, and someone else sees to it. But where do you think that bounty comes from? From me, that's where. I provide it. Or rather, the land provides it for me, and I distribute it to my people. That's what chieftains do . . .

". . . except that the land is about to quit providing."

The young man stared at his father. "How can that be?"

"My druid tells me the earth's gotten tired. The earth does that, he says, when she's overworked. She's going to rest now, and there is nothing he nor I nor anyone else can do about it. Our cattle will starve for lack of grass, our ovens will stand empty for lack of grain."

"How long before the earth is rested and becomes fertile again?"

"I wish I knew," Conn told his son.

"And in the meantime . . .?"

"In the meantime, unless I can think of some solution, we are going to have to get used to being poor."

Connla of the Fiery Hair had never been poor. There had always been fat meat roasting on the spit and plenty of fabric to make all the clothing he needed. He had seen the poor, of course, for in every land and time there are those who are too feckless to provide for themselves, no matter how many opportunities are offered. When the territory of old Hundred Battles groaned with rich harvest and all one had to do to eat an apple was kick a tree, there were still men who kicked the wrong tree, or did not feel like kicking any tree. And such men invariably had lean, whining wives and children whose eyes were too big for their skulls.

Connla had seen such people, but never expected to join their ranks. "Do you mean we shall be *hungry?*"

His father sighed. "It could happen. But I will not let it happen; I will do something."

For the first time in his life Connla heard doubt in his father's voice, so he was not as reassured as he should have been.

The old chieftain made a valiant effort. Summoning together his stoutest warriors he raided nearby tribes and brought home their cattle to replenish his failing herds, and for a while there was still fat meat on the spit. Then came a day when there were no cattle to be taken within a day's march, and Conn's neighbors became so savagely defensive it was hardly worth raiding them, since more men died than the tribe could spare. A tribe that means to support itself by raiding must have plenty of strong, healthy warriors.

And strong, healthy warriors have to have enough food to eat. In the spring it became obvious that the crops would be even worse than the year before. As if suffering under a curse, the land shrank in on itself and refused to yield.

"Is that it?" Conn demanded of his druid. "Are we cursed?"

"I think not, aside from the curse we have brought on ourselves by demanding too much for too long."

"You keep saying that, but it doesn't help anything!" Conn raged at him.

Hundred Battles stalked around his fortress, looking for something to kick. A lean hound slunk around the corner of a building, ears flattened against its skull. Every rib showed. At sight of Conn, the dog growled, for it had a bone it was not about to surrender to anyone.

The old chieftain lashed out with a savage foot and the hound yelped in pain.

At once, Connla Fiery Hair ran up, his eyes accusing. "Why did you kick my dog? He wasn't hurting you!"

"Oh, is that your dog? Then I suppose you are the one who gave him a perfectly good bone, eh? I tell you, no more bones to no more dogs. Any bones we have must be boiled until they fall apart in the pot and every drop of the soup drunk by people. Dogs will have to fend for themselves. Don't you dare let me catch you throwing the smallest uneaten scrap to that miserable animal." He stalked away, muttering indignantly under his breath.

The young man stared after his father. "But—but you always liked dogs," he said to the wind, since the old man was already out of earshot.

His hound crept up to him and pressed against his knee, trembling. He patted the silky head and played idly with its soft ears. "When did you start cowering?" he asked the animal. "You never used to do that." The dog whined.

Once poverty had made a breach in the walls it came in at the gallop. Traders arrived in summer, as was their custom, but the people of Conn of the Hundred Battles had very little to trade, and were not able to get in return the goods they were accustomed to having. They looked with envious eyes at the piles of linen and furs, the beautifully carved little wooden boxes of salt, the jars of spices. When they offered what little they had been able to produce, the traders sneered. "We can do better across the river," the traders said, packing up their goods and moving on.

By this time, Conn's senior wife had been a year in her bed and showed no signs of getting up. Unlike the rest of the tribe, she was getting fat—from long inactivity and because as senior wife she was entitled to the best of whatever food there was.

She called her firstborn son to her bedside. Smiling at the beautiful young man, she said, "Connla, your father is failing. We all see it. Someday you will have to take his place. When that time comes I know you will be able to accomplish what he has not and will restore prosperity to the tribe. I want you to remember me then, and see that I have a nice house of my own and . . ."

"I am not ready to be a chieftain!" Connla protested.

"Of course not, of course not, you are still young." she said hastily. "And the old man has a few seasons left in him. I just want you to be prepared for the inevitable, that's all. Think about it. Observe your father and decide what you will do differently."

So Connla began following his father around and watching him. He did not learn much, for Hundred Battles was not doing very much. He visited farmers and exhorted them to plant more crops, but they laughed at him as they pointed to their depleted soil. "Why should we put more seed into the earth just to watch it die?" they demanded to know. So Conn went to his herders and urged them to find richer pasturage for the cattle, but they merely shrugged. "We've taken them into every field and meadow, but still they grow thin. We could go across the river, where the grass is still good, but the tribe who holds that land is larger than ours and would slaughter us all."

Watching, Connla could not decide what answer his father should make to them.

The faces of the people began to lose color, to grow pale and thin. Even the old chieftain had to put a new notch in his belt, because one day when he stood up the weight of his sword dragged the belt off his hips. An air of gloom hung over the Hill of Usna like a storm cloud, and everyone waited for the storm to break.

It did, with a vengeance.

One morning just after dawn an army came marching across the river and attacked the stronghold of Conn of the Hundred Battles. It had become common knowledge throughout the region that Conn's warriors were underfed and their weapons needed replacing, so his neighbors came gladly to rob him while he was in a weakened condition. They took his seed bulls and his best chariot horses and the once-plump, still provocative daughters of Fionn the Smith, and they left Conn's warriors beaten and bloody.

He had won a hundred battles but now he had lost one. The old chieftain was furious. Fighting side by side with his warriors throughout the day, he had slain his share of the raiders but had not been able to stem their tide. As darkness fell, he sat morosely atop his hill and surveyed the horizon. The word would be quickly passed, he knew: Conn can be beaten.

He heard a sound behind him. At once his hand went to his sword hilt.

"It's me, Father, Connla."

"Oh. Well, come and sit down. Take a good look at this land while it is still ours, for one day we may be driven away from here and have to go live in a bog someplace." The old man sighed. His hair was no longer the color of a snow-frosted fox pelt, but had gone totally white. He looked at his youthful son and wondered if he had ever felt that young, that strong and comfortable in his body.

A cold wind blew and the joints of Hundred Battles ached in protest.

"Tomorrow," he said slowly, without enthusiasm, "we will have to count our losses and repair our weapons, because soon we must fight again. Every man of us must be armed and ready, Connla. That includes you. You have practiced with sword and shield and I know how quick you are. You will make a good warrior."

But Connla had seen the ruin of the battlefield. He had gone with the others to help carry in the dead, and had seen the puddles of blood soaking into the earth and heard men screaming in pain. When he was a little boy and his father the greatest of heroes, he had thought battle synonymous with glory. Now he knew different. Battle was the prelude to horror.

"I have no desire to be a warrior, Father," he said. It was the bravest act of his young life.

The old chieftain leaped to his feet with blazing eyes. He was so shocked, so angry, that for a moment he was incoherent. "What are you saying! I cannot believe a son of mine would ever utter such words! You have gone mad, you are ill, lie down where you are and I will call a physician to heal you . . ."

"I am not mad, nor ill, Father," Connla interrupted. His voice was deep and overrode his father's rantings. "I will gladly serve the tribe in any other way I can, but I have no desire to leave my guts spread out all over the earth for nothing." He put it as bluntly as he could to make his father listen.

Conn stared at him. He could not believe this glorious youth, the finest of his offspring, could be reluctant to take up arms. They came of warrior stock for a hundred generations! "You are only talking like this because you are dispirited," Conn finally managed to say. "I know things have been very bad here for a while, but they will get better, you'll see. The druid assures me the earth eventually rests herself enough to become productive again, and when that happens and everyone has enough food in their bellies, we will be stronger than any other tribe. This is just a temporary setback, boy."

Hundred Battles put his arm around his son's shoulders and gave him a rough hug. "This is just a mood you're in, eh? Eh? It will pass." He squeezed again. "Come now, we'll go into the hall and look in the bottoms of all the wine jars. We'll find some dregs we can drink, and put some twigs on the fire, and be ourselves again, eh?"

Connla let himself be cajoled into the hall, and he sat quietly there while his father regaled him with old war stories and optimistic plans for the future. But mostly he just stared into the fire and wondered what the future really held.

Two

EVERYTHING HAD CHANGED. Once, the reputation of Hundred Battles had been sufficient to hold other chieftains back from his borders, but now, it seemed, a new battle must be fought every other fortnight. Sometimes they were small border skirmishes, but sometimes they were terrible struggles that lasted for days, involving many men and numerous casualties. Conn used every morsel of skill and cunning he possessed just to keep from being completely overrun while he watched his borders being nibbled away.

When he managed a victory, he captured the enemy warriors and tried to recruit them into his own army, making extravagant promises he had little hope of keeping. Some of the warriors did stay with him, as a result of dissatisfaction with their own chieftains or lands or wives, but they were not a trustworthy lot. When a better offer came along they would cheerfully desert and Conn knew it.

His own children were a different matter. They must stay with him. Connla of the Fiery Hair had grown so tall and strong, in spite of the food shortage, that he would be worth three men in combat. Yet he still had no taste for battle. Sometimes his father looked at his first wife, lying fat and demanding in her bed, and wondered if his oldest son was really his.

His other boys were growing to manhood and taking their places in the ranks of the fighting men, and as the situation grew more desperate even Fiery Hair was at last forced by his own conscience to join them. He could not do otherwise and remain an honorable man.

A proud day that was for his father. The land was impoverished, the tribe was one step away from rebelling against his authority and selecting a new chieftain, but on the day his oldest son finally agreed to become a warrior, Conn of the Hundred Battles felt like a new man. He drank so much wine and sang so many war songs he awoke the next morning with an exploding head and a throat like raw meat.

He did not care. Life was good again, his son would take up where he left off.

Ignoring his pounding headache, the old chieftain was struggling into his clothes when his druid came to him. As usual, Coran simply materialized. One moment, he was not there—and in the next moment, he was. It could have been that Hundred Battles was growing deaf and just did not hear his approach, but no one dared suggest such a possibility.

"You are sending your son out today, to meet the sons of Owen on the battlefield."

"I am."

Coran drew himself up to his full height. "Then be warned, my chieftain. When you force a man to do the job for which he is not fitted, you pull awry all the threads that weave his destiny!"

Hundred Battles glared at his druid. "Why is it you never have good news for me anymore?"

"I would bring you good news," Coran said, "if you were doing good things. But . . ."

"Out of my sight!" roared his chieftain. And then, to his servants, "Send my oldest son to me at once. I want him to carry my sword and shield into battle so he will do our family honor!"

When Connla stood before his father, the young man kept his eyes cast down. His posture was that of the stolid ox that knows it must serve but does so with no passion for the task. "Make me proud of you, boy," Hundred Battles kept saying to him. "Make me proud of you."

The army marched out to meet the latest enemy, and young Connla of the Fiery Hair was in the front rank. He had been well trained, he knew the sword work and the footwork. He knew just when to lift his shield and when to lower it to throw his javelin. All these things he did at the right time, in the right way . . . and, to his surprise, he was still alive at the end of the day.

Not only that, but the enemy had been the first to leave the field of battle.

"You were victorious!" his comrades assured him, pounding him on the back. "We followed your red hair like a flame leading us onward and you led us right through the enemy lines. Their leader is dead, their loot is ours. Tomorrow we will attack again and drive the rest of them from this land. Then, if you will go with us, we will launch a new campaign against the next set of invaders."

Connla returned to his father's stronghold with a weary heart. He had not enjoyed the fighting, or the killing. When men all around him were screaming, he had attacked with a quiet, deadly efficiency, just wanting it to be over so he could leave the scene. He did not look at the men he killed and did not join in stripping them of their gold and weapons.

He felt sick inside when he considered the future, and the knowledge that he must fight again.

That night he was toasted in his father's banquet hall and he smiled and bowed, but made no victory speeches. Connla did not feel he had won anything.

Yet step by step, he and the men who followed him drove the invaders out of their territory. Then they followed the enemy across the border into their own lands and relieved them of cattle and slaves and gold, bringing the treasure back to the Hill of Usna. Bards began composing mighty epics in honor of the fighting son of Hundred Battles, a man they predicted would be a greater warrior than even his father.

Connla stood in the doorway of his father's hall and gazed out at the misty land, wishing things could be as they had once been.

"Tomorrow," his father announced, "there will be no fighting. For as far as I can see, there is no stranger on our soil. So tomorrow we will celebrate by building a great bonfire on the hill and roasting our enemy's cattle, and there will at last be singing and merriment again in my land."

"A bonfire will attract attention," Coran warned. "Some new invaders may come, drawn by its light."

Conn of the Hundred Battles shrugged. "What if they do? I have a strong son who will soon drive them away again. Eh? Eh?" He pounded his son on the shoulder and cackled with glee, feeling almost young again himself. Surely the tide had turned, and the next crop of grain would sprout. The next spring's grass would be rich and nutritious again.

So the bonfire was built to the chieftain's order and his people danced around it, singing. They made wreaths of holly to adorn young Connla and gave him a carved stick of ash, its design gilded with enemy gold. He smiled and nodded and thanked them; he did all the proper things. But his eyes were sad.

In the morning the whole hill reeked of the dead ashes of the bonfire. Hundred Battles took his oldest son with him when he went out to inspect the scene and look at the land beyond, in case there was some sign of invasion. The wind sang around them on the hilltop, it picked up ashes and swirled them into graceful shapes, it blew sweetly as if it had never crossed scorched earth where men lay dead.

As Conn spoke of the next battle, the next victory, his son watched the ashes blow. Suddenly he straightened and peered harder, then shook his head as if he had seen nothing.

The wind blew, the ashes danced, and he looked again. This time he rubbed his eyes.

Coming toward him through the swirling ash he saw a young woman. She was dressed in strange clothing that glittered when she walked—if she was indeed walking. Her gait was more like the soaring of a bird in the air or the gliding of a salmon in a pool, she was that graceful. And her face was unlike any Connla had seen in his lifetime.

She came straight up the hill toward him, her eyes fixed on his. Glossy black was her hair, curling all around her face. Very white was her skin, like skin that never sees the sun. She was tiny, no higher than Connla's heart, and that same heart went out to the young woman the moment he saw her. "Who are you?" he asked in a whisper as she came up to him.

The girl smiled. "You may call me Blathine," she said. "In your language it means a little flower."

"Is not my language your language?" the boy asked in wonder.

"It is not, for I come from a very different place."

Connla was enraptured by her beauty and the soft-
ness of her voice. She spoke so low he had to lean forward to catch her words, yet every word was pure and
distinct. His eyes drank in her beauty, from her round
white arms to the high insteps of her tiny feet in their
silver slippers. No one in his father's land knew how to
tan leather as soft as the leather in those shoes. No one in
his father's land looked like Blathine.

"Tell me about the place you come from," Connla
urged her. "Are there others there like you?"

She laughed, a sweet silvery cascade of sound as delicate as the bluebells blooming on the hillside. "Where I
come from, everyone is like me," she said. "It is a beautiful place in all seasons. No one dies there, neither man
nor woman, tree nor flower. Every day is a festival and
we have everything we could possibly want. We sing
and laugh and play games; we never say farewell to
friends or have to shrink from enemies."

"Are your people cattlemen? Or plowmen? How do you
feed and clothe yourselves? Whence comes your wealth?"

"Ah, the source of our wealth is the land where we
live, for we cherish our earth and she is good to us in
return. We call our homeland the Isles of the Blest and it
is a place of very great magic."

"Such things cannot be," Connla said in amazement.

"Can they not? But I am here to tell you they are
real!" Her eyes flashed. Dark eyes they were, like the sky
on a starless night.

A few paces away Conn of the Hundred Battles stood
talking with the captain of his guard, a red-faced, heavy-
jowled man with a voice as gruff as his disposition. They
were discussing the strengthening of fortifications
around the chieftain's stronghold and paying little attention to what went on around them. But the voice of
Blathine, as sheer and silvery as starshine, somehow cut
through their conversation.

"What's that?" said the old chieftain. "Who spoke?"

Ronan, his captain, glanced around. "I heard no one."

"Listen . . . there it is again."

"That's the wind."

Hundred Battles frowned. "I could have sworn . . ." Then he noticed his son in animated conversation with empty space. The chieftain's jaw sagged.

"Connla!" he called. "Who are you talking to?"

The young man turned. "Her name is Blathine," he said. There were two red spots burning on his cheeks.

"Whose name is Blathine? What are you saying, boy? I see no one."

Connla turned back and there was the girl, smiling at him. "But she's right here beside me."

His father took a step forward, looking perplexed. "There is no one beside you."

Ronan let out a low, frightened exclamation. "He's going mad!"

Conn whirled upon him. "Don't ever say that. There is nothing wrong with my son; he's perfect."

"But he's talking to someone who isn't there."

"Someone is there," the chieftain insisted. "I told you I heard a voice." No sooner had he said the words than it came again, the sheer and silvery sound.

Laughing, Blathine called out to him, "You son is speaking to the representative of a kingdom without aging or death, without poverty or hunger. What have you to offer him better than that, old man?"

He could not be certain he heard her, yet Conn felt a chill touch his heart. The voice had no body, it might be only illusion. He hoped it was illusion, for it frightened him.

"Go away!" he ordered as fiercely as if he were still in the strength of youth.

Blathine laughed again. This time Hundred Battles could hear her very clearly. "You cannot drive me away as long as your son wants me. If I leave, I will take him with me to the Isles of the Blest, the Plains of Pleasure, for that is where he truly belongs."

"You will not take him anyplace!" screamed Conn of the Hundred Battles. He shook his gnarled old fists at the empty air.

Ronan, who had still heard nothing but a peculiar sighing of the wind, looked from the father to the son and shook his head. "They're both going mad," he muttered. "This is a sad day for us indeed."

Blathine turned back to Connla and ran one small, slender hand across his fiery hair. "Come with me," she said softly. "You are so beautiful, so flushed with life. Your skin is ruddy and bright and your heat warms me as I have not been warmed for a very long time. Come with me and we will do nothing but dance and celebrate, day after day."

"Does anyone ever die in battle on these islands of yours?"

"No one ever dies in battle there," she promised him solemnly.

"And would we have far to go to get there?"

"Not too far. If you look toward the setting sun, you will see our pathway. Come now, I will guide you." She tugged at his arm just as Conn rushed up and grabbed his son by the other arm.

"I don't know what is happening, but you must pay no attention," he said urgently to Connla. "If you are hearing voices, they are evil ones; close your mind to them. Tell yourself they are not real." Even as he spoke these words, Hundred Battles realized his own mind had closed against the seductive, silvery voice, and he could no longer hear it. A sense of relief washed over him.

But his son still had that intense, listening expression on his face.

"Come with me," the old chieftain urged a little more gently. "Come now."

"Come now," echoed Blathine. "Come with me and never look back."

"Do you not hear her?" Connla asked his father. "Can you not see her? She is so very beautiful, and she comes from a land of enchantments."

"That is no land for you!" Hundred Battles roared. "I need you!"

"And I need to find a better place than this," his son told him. "A land of peace and happiness, where I will not have to fight anymore. I am so tired of fighting. I want no one else's blood on my hands."

"Utter nonsense and total rubbish," his father told him. "A land of peace indeed. No land has peace for very long, because it is the way of life to struggle for existence. How well could we survive if we never fought? We would soon grow as weak as that miserable spindly grain in our fields. No, Connla, fighting is a necessity because it makes a man tough and resilient and proves who is better."

"It doesn't have to be that way," whispered Blathine. Even to Connla, her voice seemed to be fading. He tried to shake off his father's grip on his arm but the old man hung on with all the tenacity he possessed. A swirl of windblown ash from the bonfire sprang up around them, and when it subsided the girl was gone.

Connla of the Fiery Hair called her name once, pleadingly, and then again. But there was no answer at all.

"You have a fever," his father told him. "That's the problem. Come with me, we'll go inside and you can lie down. I'll have the women make poultices for your chest and potions for your belly and you'll feel better soon."

"But I felt wonderful just a moment ago! When *she* was here."

Hundred Battles shook his head. "She was never here. You were dreaming with your eyes open. Help me with him, Ronan." Together, the two of them got Connla into the bedchamber and forced him to lie down. The women came to cluck over him and everyone walked around him on tiptoe, thinking him ill.

But Connla knew he was not ill. Since he had no choice he surrendered to their care, knowing their potions and poultices could never drive the memory of Blathine from him. He had seen her once; he would see her again.

His father watched him out of the corner of his eye. He noted the way Connla gazed off into space, and gave absent-minded answers to the most simple questions. Sometimes he did not answer at all, but appeared to be listening intently to . . . something else.

"It is definitely some form of enchantment," Hundred Battles decided. "Fearing the strength of my next generation, one of my enemies has had his own druids cast spells on the boy, to weaken him. Well, I have my own druids and I will match them spell for spell! They shall not take my strongest weapon from me!"

Sending for Coran and his acolytes, Hundred Battles ordered them to return to the site of the bonfire and perform whatever rituals were necessary to throw up a screen that no foreign magic could penetrate.

At dawn Coran went to the site, accompanied by six younger members of the priesthood. They wore heavy robes of woven fabric, with great hoods pulled well over their faces so that no one could catch their eyes and seize their wills. In their hands they carried the most potent symbols—of hazel and ash and mistletoe—and as they walked they chanted spells in the archaic, forgotten tongue only druids knew.

The sky darkened with every step they took and every word they said.

The hillside with its burned branches and cold ashes was a lonely place. Coran and his troop circled it seven times, walking in the sunwise direction. From a little jug that he carried, Coran sprinkled water on the dead ashes of the fire. The water had been taken from a spring sacred to the water goddess, and used with the appropriate charms it was very powerful. Sprinkling it upon the ashes should keep any other druids from using Hundred Battles' fire as a target for their own magical workings.

Lastly, Coran stood at the crest of the hill and raised his arms. Throwing back his head with its wild mane, he shrieked aloud in a voice that could melt stone. "Whatever you are, you are not welcome here!" he cried, "and if you return, the sun will burn you, the sea will drown you, the earth will open and swallow you up!"

Satisfied that he had done all that was necessary, Coran beckoned to his acolytes and they went back to their chieftain's stronghold for thanks and a feast.

And in due time, young Connla's fever abated and he seemed himself again. He was still not eager for battle, but his abilities were as outstanding as ever and the men followed him to new victories. But sometimes, when evening turned the air blue and a hush settled over the land, he did appear to be listening.

And one day his vigil was rewarded.

Returning from a skirmish at a ford on the perimeter of his father's territory, Connla and his men were making their way home through an orchard. For several years this particular stand of trees had borne no fruit, being old and gnarled and weary. When Connla entered this grove he stopped suddenly and cocked his head, holding out one hand to halt the men behind him. "Hush!" he ordered. "Do you hear her calling me?"

"Hear who? What?"

"Be quiet!" he commanded. Then he smiled, for Blathine came toward him through the green leaves, shimmering like light on wet grass.

"You are hungry," she said to Connla alone. No one else heard her; no one else saw her.

"I am," he agreed. "We have come a long way without eating. But when I see you I forget about food."

"Ah, you must eat," she laughed, and with a wave of her wrist she suddenly held out an apple to him, an apple so round and plump it surely never came from the ancient trees nearby. Yet when he looked they were all heavy with apples. "This is for you," Blathine said. "Eat nothing else until I come to you again."

The wind sighed, the trees shivered, and she was gone. The orchard was as bare as before. But in his hand Connla held one solitary, perfect apple.

His men looked uneasily at one another. "Who was he talking to?" they asked. "And where did he get that fruit?" "Is there none for us?"

He was uncomfortable eating the apple in front of them, so he dropped it into the top of his tunic, and the belt around his waist kept it in place. But from time to time his stomach cried out for just one bite, and he withdrew the apple surreptitiously and bit a chunk out of it.

No fruit had ever tasted so sweet, so juicy. Yet each time he took out the apple for another bite he found it whole again, the preceding bite healed. He ate again, and again, and there was never any less apple than before.

When they reached his father's stronghold the other warriors hurried to the feasting hall to celebrate their latest victory, but Connla went off by himself and feasted on his apple.

In time, of course, his father noticed that Connla Fiery Hair was not sitting in his customary place at the banquet table. He sent for his son and demanded his presence. Connla came, but refused both food and drink.

"He's getting sick again," Hundred Battles muttered to himself. "You over there . . . fetch my physician at once!"

Declan the Healer came at the run. He felt Connla's forehead and looked at his tongue, he put his head against the boy's chest and listened to the solid, reliable thump of his heart. He even bit off a lock of the fiery hair and chewed it. But he could find no sign of illness.

"This young man is immensely strong and very well-nourished," he reported to the chieftain.

"He eats nothing, how can he be well-nourished? I am afraid he will waste away, and if he does, hard times will come back to this land."

Declan shrugged. "He does not look as if he is in much danger of wasting away. And he does eat; I saw him take a bite out of a magnificent apple."

"Hunh!" snorted Conn. "Apples are not sufficient fare for warriors. I want to see that boy eating beef and wild boar."

So he ordered his cooks to prepare their best dishes to tempt Connla's appetite, yet the young man refused all of them, even venison simmered in wine and smothered with cream. But from time to time he was seen to take an apple from his tunic and eat a bite.

"That's it!" Hundred Battles realized. "One of my enemies has sneaked a bewitched fruit to him and means to steal his strength that way. Send Coran to me at once!"

The druid listened attentively to Conn's words, and frowned. "I don't like this," he said. "Whoever is assaulting your son with magic is a very dangerous enemy. A new enemy, because I cannot believe it is the same one that I defeated at the bonfire site."

"Are you certain?" Conn of the Hundred Battles narrowed his eyes.

"Oh, absolutely. I cast such a powerful spell that nothing could overcome it. So this magic must come from a different source, and will require a different spell. But the fact that your enemies keep trying to get at your son is alarming."

"It is indeed," Hundred Battles agreed. "I want him thoroughly protected, do you understand me? I mean *thoroughly* protected!"

This time Coran took twelve acolytes with him, and they marched all the way around the borders of the territory. At every crossroads they chanted a spell; at every spring they left an offering; at every sunrise and sunset they offered sacrifices.

Coran at last returned, looking very pleased. "Your son is quite safe now," he told his chieftain. "I am exhausted, of course, having worn myself thin in your service. But no magic, no matter how powerful, can cross your borders and attack young Fiery Hair again."

"I hope you're right," Conn told him, though privately he was beginning to have a jaundiced view of magic, no matter who practiced it. He much preferred the straightforward world of sword and spear.

The next day the old chieftain observed his son closely. In the morning the boy ate nothing. At highsun he ate nothing. In the evening he went off by himself for a little while, and when he came back into the hall for the night's feasting he ate nothing.

Hundred Battles was certain the boy had eaten, however. He had eaten that apple.

The only thing to do was get it away from him somehow, and the chieftain would not allow anyone but himself to lay hands on his son. So the next day he announced they would go to the Plain of Arcomin to observe a chariot race being held there, the two of them together. A pleasant outing for father and son it would be, in an atmosphere of high good humor.

Surely, old Hundred Battles told himself, there would come some moment when he could hug Connla and, under cover of the embrace, get his hands on that apple.

A great circular racecourse was maintained on the
Plain of Arcomin, exclusively for chariot racing. The
people loved this sport above all others, and even tribes
at war with one another would come together peacefully
on race day to contest their best teams and drivers. So a
great crowd had gathered around the racecourse to enjoy
the event, and there was much laughter and wagering,
much embracing and backslapping and rough good humor.

Conn of the Hundred Battles scanned each face he
saw, wondering which of them was trying to enchant
and weaken his son.

Fiery Hair looked at faces, too, thinking to himself
that none of them was the right face. This one was too
plump, that too thin, the other too ruddy. One woman's
hair was too pale and another's too thin. Blathine was not
anywhere in the crowd. Yet he could not stop looking for
her. He would never stop looking for her.

He patted his tunic and felt her apple safe inside,
snug against his heart.

Conn of the Hundred Battles took his place among the
other chieftains of major tribes, assembled to enjoy the
racing. A high wooden platform had been built for them,
and each man had stationed his personal guard near the
steps, just in case. But they came together with smiles for
one another and a great air of jollity—plus much boast-
ing about the horses each chieftain had brought to race.

Conn insisted that his oldest and favorite son join him
on the chieftains' platform, and the others made room for
Fiery Hair. They knew who he was; his band of soldiers
had been making a name for themselves in battles against
their own warriors. He was the new young weapon of
Hundred Battles and must be treated with respect until
his measure was taken.

Sitting among them on carved wooden benches,
Connla was quietly observing them too. He saw men who
were far from carefree, as this occasion was not a carefree

occasion. No lighthearted festival, this race, but another way of competing and defeating. Someone would win but many would lose. There was a low, nasty roar from the crowd, which indicated the people were eager to see someone go down in defeat.

The race, when it began, was savage. The chariots were lined up wheel to wheel, and at a given signal the air crackled with whips snapping. Horses plunged forward with a mighty creaking of cart and axle. Charioteers slammed their vehicles against each other as they fought for the best positions.

"There is my team, the driver wears a blue tunic!" Hundred Battles exulted. "And look at that, he has already driven one chariot clear off the racecourse and into the shrubbery."

The chariots thundered over the earth, creating a vivid spectacle. Made of wickerwork, they were decorated with painted shields and dyed plumes in brilliant colors, and their iron wheels had been polished to a blue gleam. The hubs of the wheels were set with curved blades, like scythes, and when one chariot got close enough to another, those blades could sever wheel spokes. As Connla watched, several chariots were destroyed this way in the early part of the race, spilling men out onto the earth. But the horses ran on and the yelling grew louder.

The chariots swept around the circular track in a cloud of yellow dust. Arms upraised to whip the horses emerged from the cloud and disappeared again. A cart suddenly shot out of the clattering herd, one wheel broken, and lurched drunkenly onto the grassy verge. When it tipped over, its horses panicked and kicked the wickerwork to pieces as the charioteer tried desperately to crawl clear before some other racer ran over him.

Hundred Battles and his fellow chieftains were screaming at their drivers, shouting instructions that no

one could hear in the general tumult. The overall sound
had become one great, bloodthirsty roar, with no single
syllable distinguishable from any other.

Then, above it all, Connla heard a silvery tinkle of
laughter.

He sat up very straight. His father had not noticed; no
one seemed to hear it but himself.

"Blathine! Is that you?" He looked around eagerly,
but he did not see her. There was nothing to be seen but
the hysterical crowd and the horses sweeping around the
last curve to the finish line, white foam streaked with
blood on their satiny hides, eyes rolling and wild, drivers out of control with their desire to win at whatever
cost. The air was thick with curses as men lashed their
whips at each other, and the deadly scythes cut through
first one wheel and then another, causing dreadful
wrecks.

"This is a monstrous spectacle," said a soft voice in
Connla's ear. "Come away with me and I will show you
better games, kinder games. Games where neither man
nor animal dies."

Connla whirled on his bench and there she stood behind him, smiling down at him. In that violent, screaming crowd she was very small and fragile, yet no one
shoved her. No one seemed aware of her at all but
Connla.

She held out her hands to him. "Come now," she
urged. "They will never miss you."

He felt a sudden warmth within his tunic where her
apple lay against his heart. The fruit began to pulse as if
it had a life of its own. A groan of pleasure escaped
Connla's lips and somehow his father heard it.

The old chieftain turned to look at his son. "What's
the matter, you're not watching the race!"

Connla did not answer. Indeed, he was not aware of
his father or the race or anything but Blathine. The two

red spots were burning on his cheeks again and his eyes were unnaturally bright.

Hundred Battles felt a stab of alarm. "Boy? Boy!" He grabbed his son's arm just as Blathine put one of her tiny white hands on that same arm . . . and, for a moment, Conn of the Hundred Battles could see her very clearly. He looked straight into a face that froze him with terror.

Three

THE OLD CHIEFTAIN reeled backward, flailing his hands in the air as if to fight off some unseen enemy. The men around him caught him instinctively and kept him on his feet, else he would have fallen. Even Connla's attention was captured and he reached out, trying to steady his father.

Hundred Battles was helped onto his bench, where he sat muttering to himself and wiping his brow. His son, concerned, bent over him. "What is it, what happened?"

"I saw her . . . that thing that wants to take you from me. That sorceress, that witch . . ." He was very pale and his eyes bulged from his head. Cold beads of sweat ran down his face. Even after his most savage battle Conn had never looked that way. "Take me home," he said in a hoarse voice to his son. "Take me away from here at once."

"But the race, don't you want to see the end of it?"

"I care not how it ends. Take me home."

"*Your* home is with me," said a voice in Connla's ear. "Leave him here where he belongs and come to your true place in the Isles of the Blest."

The young man was mightily torn. Her voice was tender and irresistible, and the kingdom she described was perfectly shaped to his heart's requirement. Yet he loved his father, and the old man was all but helpless with shock. Connla struggled with himself for a long moment, then put his arm around the sagging shoulders of Hundred Battles. "I will help you, Father. Can you stand?"

"You are a good son and a kind man," Blathine whispered in his ear. "I love you all the more for your virtues. Go, then, and care for the old man. I will wait for you. I will come for you again, fear not, my beautiful hero with the fiery hair." Her laughter tinkled and rippled and faded away.

Father and son returned to their stronghold together, leaving the joyous carnage of the racecourse behind them. Indeed, old Conn's chariot had finished second, but they did not know it. The youth's thoughts were too much with Blathine, and the old man was weak and sick.

When they reached the hall, Hundred Battles had to be helped to his own bedchamber, where he collapsed with one forearm thrown across his eyes. "Stay by me, Connla," he ordered his son. "Stay close by me."

The physician was summoned, and hard on his heels came the chief druid, Coran. By that time Hundred Battles had begun to regain his strength and was sitting up again, issuing commands. As soon as he saw his druid, the chieftain told his son to leave the two of them alone for a moment.

"I have seen the enchantment meant for my boy and it is a powerful one," Conn said. "If I were younger I could not resist her myself, yet she terrifies me."

"Why? Is she so hideous?"

"Not at all; she is exquisitely beautiful. Too beautiful. She is not mortal, and if my son gives himself over to her, he will not be mortal either. That is her attraction, I think; she wants to turn him into something like herself, not a warrior but one of the Undying Ones. The magic people, the fairy folk. They steal human babies and leave changelings in their place as everyone knows, Coran. And now this creature means to steal my own son from me as well, and leave me with nothing. He is the hope of the tribe and she wants to take him from me."

"She cannot take him against his will," Coran assured the old chieftain.

"Have you seen his face? He wants to go with her more than he ever wanted to be with me. Do something, *do something*!"

Coran the Druid had just about exhausted his assortment of things to do in such a situation, but the look on the face of Hundred Battles warned him he had better think of one more. And it had better work.

"We must call upon all the gods of war to stand by us, if we are to hold onto this young warrior of yours," Coran said. "And the gods do not give their aid cheaply."

"Whatever they demand I will pay. I cannot lose my son."

Coran nodded. "Very well, then. I will order wicker baskets built and we will offer sacrifices, but they cannot be just any sort of sacrifice. No criminals you would burn anyway, nothing like that. A sacrifice sufficient to get the attention of the gods and command their respect must be something—someone—of value."

"And that will do it?" Conn asked eagerly. "If I give you someone of sufficient value for the sacrifice, will the gods aid us in overcoming the magic that threatens to enslave my son?"

Coran nodded again, very slowly and solemnly. "I would stake my reputation on it," he said.

"You have just done so," Hundred Battles told him. "Now, name the sacrifice."

"It is for you to choose."

"A slave, then. A strong, healthy one with a lot of work in him?"

"Not good enough."

"An enemy warrior, someone of noble rank?"

"Not good enough. Remember, you are fighting for your own son. The sacrifice you offer must be of equal value."

Conn of the Hundred Battles furrowed his forehead in deep thought. Who could be of equal value to his son?

At that moment, his senior wife yelled for the tenth time that day, demanding fresh water and honey from the comb and someone to rub her back.

Coran's eyes met those of the old chieftain.

"Not her, I cannot!"

"Nothing less will do," Coran insisted, feeling pleased at the neat twist of fate that had given him such a chance to exercise his power. A druid who could get his chieftain to sacrifice his own wife must be recognized throughout druidry as having tremendous power indeed.

"No chieftain has ever ordered his own wife to the fire," Conn said. "Better you ask me to cut off my own hands at the wrists."

She yelled again, louder this time, demanding a comb for her hair and an additional coverlet for her bed and someone to hang a rug to screen off a draft that bothered her.

"Well . . ." said Conn of the Hundred Battles.

"Desperate times demand desperate measures," the druid told him.

"They do. They do indeed," Conn agreed. The flesh of his face sank into sad folds from which it would never entirely recover. "She was young and cheerful once. Such a laugh she had! She does not laugh now. I no longer recognize in her the maiden I married. I suppose the most important thing is to protect my son, and who better to protect him than the spirit of the woman who gave him birth?" To his credit, he sighed, for the thing sat heavily on him.

In the dark of night, silent men crept into the royal sleeping chamber and tied the senior wife with stout rope. They stuffed a cloth soaked in an infusion of herbs in her mouth and carried her away in a large bag. The herbs made her groggy; she did not realize she was being taken to the Hill of Fires, where a wicker cage awaited her dazed eyes as the first rays of the sun stained the sky red.

Connla lay sleeping, lost in a dream of Blathine. The dream was so real he thought he heard her voice, then realized it was in fact her voice. "Violence is being done to your mother, my love!" she cried.

He sat up in bed, rubbing his eyes. "The Hill of Fires," the silvery starshine voice told him urgently. "Hurry!"

Leaping out of bed, Connla was running before his feet touched the ground. A guard, startled by the sudden appearance of a running man, challenged him and tried to catch him, but he knocked the guard aside with one sweep of his arm and ran on.

He reached the foot of the traditional hill of bonfires in time to see flame climbing into the sky, and hear a terrible scream from the wicker cage.

Coran's voice rolled like thunder. "Deities of battle, I exhort you to accept this sacrifice for the protection of Connla of the Fiery Hair! Defend him against a woman's wiles and sorcery! And you, his mother, as you enter the world of the spirits, look back on him and protect him, see all that happens to him and stand as his invisible guardian against . . ."

"Stop!" yelled Connla, plunging up the hill. His heart was hammering in his chest like a bird trying to escape a net. With great bounds his young legs carried him to

the top, but it was already too late. The screams had
stopped, the cage was collapsing into a bed of glowing
coals.

Connla turned his eyes away and wept.

The druid finished the last details of the ritual and
hurried to the young man. "You must understand, it is
what your mother would have wanted to do. She will
protect you now from the monster."

"You are the monster," Connla told him bitterly. "You
are infinitely more dangerous and cruel than a pack of
foam-mouthed wolves." He bowed his head again and
stood in agonized silence.

Up the hill behind him came Conn of the Hundred
Battles. Strong though he was, the old chieftain had not
been able to witness the moment of sacrifice, but now he
approached his son and tried to put his arm around the
young man's shoulders. "You don't understand," he said.
"This was done to save you."

"Save me from what?" Connla threw back his head
and glared at his father out of red-rimmed eyes. "From a
beautiful girl who loves me? From the promise of a land
where no one suffers? Father, Blathine offers me endless
joy and you offer me the chance to fight and die, kill or
be killed, to hold together a kingdom for a man who ordered my own mother slain when he got tired of her."

"It isn't like that at all!" Conn protested. "The druid
said we must have a very specific type of sacrifice to protect you. I was following the advice of the *priest*, my son.
I had no choice."

"In the Isles of the Blest," Blathine murmured softly
into Connla's ear, "we do not cringe in obedience to druids, for we are upright folk who have not fallen out of
favor with the gods. We need no priesthood to beg on
our behalf or make cruel demands upon us. No one is
ever sacrificed in our land, Connla. Come with me now
and leave pain and the memory of pain behind."

Hundred Battles read correctly the expression on his son's face. "She is talking to you right now, isn't she? Trying to work her enchantments on you? Don't listen to her, my son. Stay here where we need you."

"What about what I need?"

The druid had joined them, listening to the tides of the conversation to see which way they ran. Now he interjected, "You cannot go even if you try, Connla. My magic will override all others, for nothing is more potent than the sacrifice I offered on this hill in the sunrise." He said this defiantly, catching the old chieftain's anguished eye and demanding belief.

"Love is more potent," Blathine told Connla. "If you love me, come with me now. All you have to do is take one more bite of the apple I gave you. Its sweet juices will flood your mortal senses and make you forget mortal food, mortal life. That apple came from the Isles of the Blest."

Reaching into his tunic, Connla took out the apple. In spite of all the times he had bitten into it, the fruit was still whole, shiny with immortality. "If it were not for the woman who just died here," he said to Hundred Battles, "I might have stayed with you. But I want no part of what you are or what you're willing to do."

"I did it for you!" his father protested.

"So much the worse, then." And Connla bit into the apple.

At once a blue-white wind came howling down out of the clear dawn sky. Whirling and spiraling it made for itself a shape, and that shape solidified into a snowy horse with a proud high crest and a long tail. The horse pawed the earth but did not stand upon it, since it floated in the air and they could all see space between its hooves and the grass.

They could see something more, for with the materialization of the horse, Blathine herself appeared, as solid

as a mortal woman. She wore a robe of silver silk fastened
with brooches of amethyst, and her black hair was bound
with fillets of silver. With one small hand she seized the
horse's bridle; her other hand reached out to Connla.
"Mount behind me," she said.

Now that the moment of decision had come, Connla
hesitated. He was not afraid of the magic, and there was
nothing in Blathine's beautiful face to frighten him. But
this was his homeland, and the man who clutched at him
and pleaded with him had been his admired father.

Seizing the opportunity, Coran the Druid rushed forward with his hazel stick held over his head. He bran-
dished it at the fairy woman and cried, "Begone, sorceress!"

The hazel has great power. Gentle friend of the ill,
enemy of fever, lovely and graceful tree, it represents
wholesomeness and healing. Life flows through the veins
of the hazel tree, mortal life. Yet, like all trees, it inhab-
its a different world from that men know, and in that
world it has its own magical properties.

So the druid threatened Blathine with his hazel wand,
and for one brief moment the spectators saw her eyes
change. Soft and brilliant those dark eyes had been,
burning with love for Connla, but just for one heartbeat
they went as flat and black as stones of polished obsidian.

In that fateful interval Connla made his choice, react-
ing to this final intervention on the part of the priest.
With a great spring he leaped up behind Blathine on the
horse and they swirled from the sight of mortal men.

Hundred Battles stood on the hilltop, beside the still-
smoldering sacrificial fire, and he stared at the receding
silver clouds. "What have you done?" he at last asked
Coran.

"I did exactly what you wanted," the druid told
him.

"But my son is gone."

"Ah . . . well. That is unfortunate."

"*Unfortunate!* I'll show you what unfortunate means, you shaggy-eared dog-dropping!" The old chieftain grabbed for his druid's throat, with murderous fingers.

At once the other druids closed around the pair and pulled Coran to safety. Hundred Battles, firmly pinioned, glared in fury. "You failed and I'll have you burned on this same hill!"

Coran shook his head. "You dare not do violence to a druid. And I did not fail. True, her magic was stronger than I anticipated, but fortunately we had concluded the sacrifice before she got him. He goes with protection now; no matter what blandishments the witch offers, he will be able to hear another voice arguing for the real world, for you and his homeland and his own people." Coran gestured to the smoldering coals of the fire. "His mother's spirit is free of its shell and surely goes with Connla Fiery Hair. In time she will pull him away from the Isles of the Blest."

"The woman probably has no great desire to do me any favors," Conn muttered.

"She might not reclaim her son for you, but she will do it for his own sake. Just give her time."

Hundred Battles was sinking deeper, moment by moment, into abject misery. "Give her time, indeed. Who will give me time? When the people find out their bright hope is gone and my finest son has deserted us, will they still support me? Or have I seen my last day as chieftain at Usna? I tried to do everything right. You know I did. As a warrior I never faltered. I shrank from no task, no hardship. I did everything as I had been trained to do it, and this is my reward. If only I could go back and begin again, I would do it differently."

The chief druid looked at him. "How would you do it differently?" he asked.

Conn of the Hundred Battles drew a deep breath. When he finally answered, his voice seemed to come from a dark, lost cave inside himself. "I do not know," he admitted.

Coran touched him, very cautiously. "This has not gone as badly as you think. Your son will return."

"Will he?" The old chieftain's eyes were bleak. "Is that all you have left to offer me from your bag of tricks, druid? Hope?"

"Hope is priceless," Coran assured him.

"Hope is what's left at the bottom of the bag," Hundred Battles said. "Like lint."

Four

A T FIRST THE swiftness of their flight took Connla's breath away. The horse and its riders were enveloped in a blue-white cloud, obscuring any sight of the land over which they soared. The young man could feel the animal's broad, warm rump beneath his buttocks, and when he wrapped his arms around Blathine's waist she felt as solid to him as any mortal woman. Yet he knew he was lost in magic.

He was a warrior's son. He did not want to admit fear. But he held Blathine very tightly, and from the rigidity of his arms she knew.

He heard her soft laugh. "I think you would be happier if you could see," she said. "We will travel lower, then." She uttered a strange combination of syllables in a language Connla did not know, and at once he felt the horse angle downward. The clouds parted and they were galloping above a green and rolling land, fragrant with blossoms.

Connla could hear the hum of bees and the distant sound of women singing at their work. In the distance he caught glimpses of red deer at the edge of a mighty forest. Again, he saw a rise of purple mountains, sweetly rose-flushed in the light of a lowering sun. They crossed the plain and the mountains, they crossed a broad river embroidered along its banks with reeds, and Connla thought he had never seen so beautiful a place.

"Are we in the Isles of the Blest?" he asked Blathine.

"Foolish boy, of course not. We are still in your own land. Do you not recognize it? We will have to cross open water to reach our destination."

Connla gazed down in wonder at the bounteous earth revealed beneath the hooves of the flying horse. "I never knew my land was this beautiful," he said.

"It appears so to you because you thought we had reached paradise, and you were all prepared to see marvels." Blathine said something else to the horse and it veered to one side. "The Isles of the Blest are better than this," she promised.

Their changed direction took them over a less luxuriant landscape of crumpled earth and stark, staring stone. Yet in this scenery, as well, did Connla find beauty, and he gazed and gazed at it as if he could never fill his eyes. I am leaving this forever, he thought. I will see it no more. And he felt a great sadness, a nostalgia for places he had never had a chance to know.

At the westernmost edge of the crumpled land a gray sea bit chunks out of the coastline. The horse leaped high into the air above this sea, galloping hard. The air seemed colder here and in spite of himself, Connla shivered.

"You will be warm as soon as we get home," Blathine assured him.

He had no way of knowing how long they had been in the air or how far they had come. Days might have passed, for sometimes a cloud rolled over them again and they could see nothing, neither light nor dark. Then the cloud would roll away and there would be only angry sea below, white-capped and sullen. He had seen lakes and rivers, but Connla had never seen an ocean, and its very size was beyond his comprehension.

"Where does it end?" he asked Blathine.

"It does not end. The ocean is everything. All the land is merely an interruption in the sea."

Her words made no sense; such things could not be possible.

Weariness overcame him and he leaned his shining red-gold head against the fairy woman's shoulder. He did not want to fall asleep for fear he might fall off and be drowned in that angry gray water far below. But though every time he felt himself drifting away he forced his eyes open again, at last they became so heavy and grainy he could resist no more.

Connla fell asleep, and the white horse drifted down to alight upon a rocky shore.

He awoke with a start. "Is this it? Are we there?"

"Of course not," Blathine told him. "Look around you. Does this place answer to my description? This is merely a stop we have to make along our way, for there is a little chore I need you to undertake for me. Passage must always be paid, even to the Isles of the Blest."

She slung one graceful leg over the horse's neck and slid to the ground. Stony ground it was, the edge of a pebbled beach devoid of any vegetation. A few sea birds wheeled overhead, and in the distance Connla could see more of them, squabbling over some morsel of carrion the sea had cast up on the shore.

"What needs doing here?"

"Just a small thing, just a little thing for someone like yourself," Blathine assured him. She smiled, and laid her tiny hand against his cheek, and Connla of the Fiery Hair felt as tall as three spears fitted end to end. "Show me what I may do for you," he said, noticing at the same time how very solid the stony beach felt beneath his feet.

"Do you see that great boulder over there, the huge chunk of granite breaking the surf into spume?"

"I do see it."

"Suppose I told you that is a giant, Connla, a brutal creature locked within stone by an enchantment. Suppose I told you further than once a year the stone softens, at midpoint of the longest day of the four seasons—and when the stone is soft enough, the giant emerges looking for prey. He will eat human flesh, my dear one, and the people who live inland are so terrified of him they leave their newborn babies here on this beach as a sacrifice so that he does not come looking for them. At sundown the enchantment takes hold again and he returns to stone, but in the meantime his appetite is terrible."

Connla was horrified. He looked down the beach again, at the birds fighting over something. Then, glancing up, he realized the sun was shining above him and had almost reached midpoint of the day.

"You want me to destroy the giant? But . . . I thought we were going to a land where there is no killing, no death, no pain!"

"This is not my homeland," Blathine reminded him. "Just a stop along the way. Still, I have friends here who are dear to me, and with a mighty warrior such as yourself I thought it a fine opportunity to free them from their misery. If you will destroy the giant, we will soon be on our way again."

Just then a groan issued from the granite boulder. As Connla watched, the stone seemed to expand, becoming soft and flexible. An arm emerged, stretching, and then another. The granite became the torso of a huge, hideously formed man, who stood up yawning. Immense, square yellow teeth were revealed in his gaping maw. His head was also square, with a coarse covering of tangled hair like seaweed, dripping to his shoulders. Tufts of hair sprouted from the back of his hands, and each hand was as big as a blackthorn club.

"Now, Connla," Blathine urged.

"But I have no weapons!" Indeed, since he had come away in only the tunic in which he had fallen asleep, young Connla had no possessions of any sort. His feet were bare and his arms were already goose-pimpled by the cold wind from the sea.

"I would not ask this of you if you could not do it," Blathine told him. She stepped backward, sheltering herself against the shoulder of her horse just as the giant turned and caught sight of them.

Letting out a roar, the creature ran down the beach toward Connla. The young man had no time to form a battle plan. He bent and seized a rock, which he threw with all his strength into the oncoming face. The stone struck a solid blow but did not even cause the giant to falter in his stride. Indeed, it merely served to madden him. In another leap he was upon Connla.

Huge fingers grabbed the fiery, silken hair. Connla felt himself being lifted into the air with excruciating pain, as if every hair on his head were being jerked from its roots. But before his own weight pulled his body free of its scalp, the giant closed his other massive paw around the young man's waist and gave him a pinch, testing to see how much fat he carried.

Warriors in fighting trim carry no fat. The giant peered myopically at his captive. This was, he realized, no morsel for a feast. He dropped the tough, lean human to the ground and growled in a voice like rocks grinding together.

Connla scrambled to his feet as quickly as he could and ducked behind a drift of stones deposited by the sea. It offered little shelter, but it felt good to have any sort of barrier between himself and the horrid creature who had almost eaten him.

The unappeased giant swung his head from side to side, sniffing the wind. Then the little pig eyes in his square skull lighted with pleasure. "*Unnh*," grunted the monster. "*Unnh-unnh-unnh!*" Forgetting Connla, he began a shambling run down the beach.

Connla saw a distant crowd depositing a bundle at the water's edge; then they turned and ran away. The giant did not pursue them but made straight for the sacrifice they had left.

Before he knew it, Connla had shouted an angry oath and was chasing the giant. He was young and lithe and his horror lent speed to his legs. He caught up with the monster just as it stooped over a baby wrapped in a shawl. Without hesitation Connla leaped into the air, snatched the infant from the giant's fingers and started to run away with it as fast as he could.

A howl of baffled fury followed him. The earth shook as the giant set off in ponderous pursuit. Connla could smell its foul breath as it panted, gaining on him with every stride.

Connla caught a glimpse of Blathine and the horse as he raced by them, but he did not dare stop. Only when he was too far away did he wonder why he had not just leaped onto the horse and urged it into the sky. Surely the magical creature could have flown off with all three of them, eluding the monster.

But it was far too late for that now. He had no option left but to run. Perhaps, if he doubled back . . .

He could not. As if it read his thoughts, the giant moved with him, blocking him. Nothing remained but a long stretch of empty beach, with the sullen sea on one hand and an increasingly sheer rise of dark cliffs on the other.

Connla was young and strong, but he was only mortal, and soon his lungs would fail him.

The baby in his arms began to wail in terror. No more sacrifices, Connla promised it silently, saving his breath for running. We will go into the sea together before I surrender you to that.

He ran on until, in all that barren landscape, something caught his eye—a glimpse of pattern that did not belong to sea and stone. A fisherman's net, torn and discarded or blown far from its rightful owner, lay cast up on the beach.

Stooping as he ran, Connla seized an edge of the net. When he glanced over his shoulder he could see how close the giant was to him. He made a desperate feint to the left and then ducked back to the right, pulling the net behind him and raising it as he ran.

One huge foot stepped into the center of the net before the giant realized what was happening. Connla jerked with all his strength. The giant lost his balance. Massive arms flailed the air. Changing direction adroitly, Connla managed to entangle the giant's feet and ankles so securely in the net that the clumsy brute could not free itself. With a crash like a tree falling, the monster measured his length on the pebble beach.

As granite, the giant was impervious to many things, but in his temporary fleshly shape he required air to breathe. The shock of hitting the ground so hard knocked all the air from his lungs with a mighty whoosh. Seeing him dazed, Connla swiftly laid the baby down and ran to get the biggest rock he could lift. He stood over the fallen monster and brought the stone down with all his force on the big square skull.

The giant rolled his eyes and raised one hand in protest, but it was too late. Connla was fighting not only for the baby's life but against his own fear. With a yell, he smashed in the giant's head.

Then he dropped his arms and stood panting.

"You killed the creature during the only time it could be killed," he heard Blathine say. "By sundown it would have become a boulder again and no simple stone could have destroyed it. Even the sea, in all these centuries, has not worn it away appreciably." She was sitting on the horse, looking down at Connla of the Fiery Hair. Her smile was sweet, her face as calm as if she had not just witnessed violence.

Connla felt drained. Turning away, he went to pick up the rescued baby . . . and found nothing but a raggedy shawl lying on the beach. It held no trace of warmth from the small body, as if there had never been a baby at all.

"Where is it?" he asked in stupefaction, looking this way and that. "Did the giant get it after all?"

"Get what?"

"The baby. The child those people left for the monster. I saved it, I want to know it is safe."

"What people?" Blathine asked him. "What monster?"

"Why, there . . ." He gestured at his fallen foe, but no great body lay cooling on the beach. There was nothing but a huge pile of tumbled stones. And no matter how he looked, he could catch no glimpse of the little group of people who had carried the baby to the beach and abandoned it.

Nothing in any direction, but stones.

Connla felt his mouth go dry. "I do not understand."

She smiled at him. "Of course not," she replied. "What is there that needs to be understood? Climb up, we have to continue our journey."

She held out her hand and Connla caught it because there was nothing else to do. He was twice her size, yet Blathine gave the gentlest little tug and easily swung him up behind her. No sooner did his legs straddle the horse than it leaped into the air and the clouds closed around them.

Connla was still breathing hard. Surely he had run a long distance. Surely he had been frightened. He could feel it in his body as his racing heart gradually slowed. Yet nothing remained but the sense of depression that follows a nightmare. Could a man die from a dream? he wondered.

"Men die for dreams," Blathine said aloud, as if she heard his thoughts, "not from them."

The horse galloped on.

The clouds parted to reveal a brilliant sun. Heat poured down on Connla's body, soaking through his thin tunic and warming him to the bone.

"We must be getting near the Isles of the Blest," he said.

"We have a little farther to go," Blathine replied.

"I suppose I'm getting anxious."

She chuckled. "You would hurry to a place where there is no time?"

"No time? Have you no seasons then, no night, no day?"

She looked over her shoulder at him and he marveled at the perfect curve of her lashes. He was so lost in contemplating their beauty that he did not think overmuch about her answer when she said, "Night is for sleeping, day is for waking. We do neither, so we have no need of night and day."

The horse galloped on.

"Look down," Blathine said.

Bending slightly, Connla noticed a disturbance in the sea below. The water had changed color and was a dark blue-green here, as if some alien current ran through it. Some sort of creatures were leaping and playing in that current.

"Are those big fish I see?"

"Not fish," Blathine told him. She gave the horse a murmured command and he flew lower until Connla could make out the details of the sea creatures. They had smooth, shining skins of silvery gray, and low dorsal fins. Their heads were blunt, with wide mouths permanently shaped into smiles. One of them suddenly rolled over onto its back and looked up at Connla.

"What are they?" he asked in astonishment. "They stay close to the surface of the water and they cavort like playful horses."

"They are dolphins," Blathine said. "A kind of whale."

"I do not know about whales."

"They know about you," she replied. "Or rather, they know about mankind. They have an infinite capacity for forgiveness. There are those who think them foolish and others who think them doomed."

"They look very gentle."

"They are. That is their trouble." She pointed one slender white finger with its perfectly shaped, pale pink fingernail. "There, that one. I think he would like to talk to you."

"I cannot talk to a fish."

"But they are not fish," Blathine corrected him. "And of course you can talk to them if you wish. And if they are willing, which does not happen very often. They rarely think humans say anything worth hearing."

The horse swooped lower still so that they were directly above the big dolphin who had rolled over on its back. It grinned up at Connla, with a smile so unquestionably benign he found himself smiling back.

"Go on, speak to him," Blathine urged.

"I am—I am Connla of the Fiery Hair, son of Conn of the Hundred Battles," he said, feeling foolish and rather wishing there were some better way to identify his father.

"You fly in the thin air," commented the dolphin, "yet you are not a bird." The creature's voice was thin and high, like piping on the wind, but Connla understood it distinctly.

"I am not flying, but riding a horse who seems to be able to fly," Connla replied. Then, curiosity made him add, "Can you see the horse and the young woman who rides with me?"

"Of course I can," the dolphin told him, grinning its perpetual grin. "I can see everything. Only humanfolk are partially blind."

Fiery Hair was stung by the insult. "My vision is perfect!"

The dolphin made a sound like laughter. "Do you think so? Tell me, then, human person: Can you see a spirit when it is not surrounded by flesh?"

"Do you mean, like a ghost? I cannot."

"Ah," said the dolphin. "Can you see the shape of the weather that is to come? Can you see its colors and patterns before it reaches you?"

"I cannot."

"And can you see the light that creatures emit when they mean to do you harm?"

"I cannot," Connla said. "Though I wish I could. That sounds a most useful ability to have."

"We have all those abilities and more besides," the dolphin told him. "As I said, only humanfolk are blind. But they probably have other gifts to make up for their deficiencies." Suddenly the creature executed a perfect roll and then leaped high into the air, forming an arc of great beauty with its sleek body. "Beware the wind!" it cried out as it plunged into the waves.

"What wind?" Connla looked around but the sky was clear, the sea calm. A more tranquil day could not be imagined.

"If the dolphin warns us, there is a storm coming," Blathine said, a note of urgency in her voice. "We must hurry on. Perhaps we can outrun it."

For the first time it occurred to Connla that her magic might have unguessable limitations. "Can't your horse fly in storms?"

She did not bother to answer, but bent low on the animal's neck and spoke into its ear. The horse responded with a mighty leap upward and began galloping furiously along whatever invisible pathway it followed through the air. Yet at every stride Blathine kicked it with her little heels and urged it to go faster. Her hair pulled loose from its silver bindings and a cascade of black curls whipped across Connla's face.

They had raced on in this manner for a timeless time before the storm caught up with them. When it did, they were attacked with a howling wind and a mighty buffeting of air currents. The horse staggered, gathered its legs under it again and went on. Yet it was obvious the animal was having difficulties. Black clouds boiled up out of the sea and surrounded them. Lightning flashed in those clouds, spears of fire hurled by angry gods at war.

Connla tightened his hold on Blathine's waist.

Though he could see nothing tangible, he could feel the effect of the unseen on the horse they rode. Sometimes it struggled up steep inclines, and at other times it seemed to plunge down invisible hills with such speed Connla's stomach turned. All the while, the storm raged around them. From time to time the clouds parted and he could catch a glimpse of the sea far below, its angry waves lashed into froth.

"Are you certain," he cried out to Blathine above the shriek of the wind, "that no one dies in the Isles of the Blest?"

"I am certain," she answered. "But we are not there yet."

At that moment a particularly powerful gust clubbed the horse and sent it staggering sideways. Connla lost his balance. He felt his fingers slip from Blathine's waist and grabbed futilely at her clothing, but it was too late. With a terrible slowness, he tumbled from the horse.

Down through the air he fell. The sea waited below, opening its hungry maw to receive him in the trough of a giant wave. His legs ran in nothingness; his arms waved wildly. Down, down he fell, and fell. And fell . . .

Until all of life seemed nothing but falling. Surely time had passed, a dreadful amount of time. He had had time to be frightened and time to take note of the various dismaying physical sensations caused by the fall. His legs had gone through their hopeless cycle of running until he realized it was doing no good and he stopped them. Still he fell. When he looked, the ocean seemed no nearer than it had before. He was suspended above it, suffering all the misery of a man falling to his death but not yet completing the plunge.

Somehow that was worse.

Throwing back his head he looked up, searching the sky for Blathine and the horse. The sky was empty. Worse, the sky was blue and clear and stormless. The black clouds that had surrounded them were gone, apparently taking the fairy woman and her mount with them.

Connla hung in the sky in horror.

When he looked down again he saw the sea gradually calming below him, returning to its customary pattern of deep, regular waves. Its color changed to a deep green, and a light seemed to shine deep down in the water, giving it a beautiful emerald translucence. But Connla got no closer to it.

He was on the brink of despair. Of all the fates he might have imagined, Connla of the Fiery Hair never expected to die of old age while hanging in the sky without any visible means of support. He was neither cold nor hot, he discovered; neither hungry nor thirsty. He was not even tired. He was just . . . there.

He looked down at the ocean again and saw movement below him. A school of dolphins approached, arcing up out of the water and diving back into it. He envied them their element, though it would be fatal to him. He needed air to breathe and he had air, but what good was it?

I have too much air, Connla thought to himself.

And then, because there was nothing else to do, he went on thinking. *If it is possible to have too much air, it is possible to have too much of anything we think of as good. There could be too much life, I suppose. Too much beauty. Too much peace.*

Suddenly he longed with all his heart for a cessation of the peace he was experiencing as he hung in the sky. To whatever random gods might be watching, he cried aloud, "Give me fear, give me terror, but let me continue my fall!"

Connla dropped out of the sky like a stone.

He had been close to the water after all, at least close enough so that he did not hit it with the impact of a man hitting something solid. Just a little of his breath was knocked out of him, but he could not breathe, anyway; he was beneath the surface. Water hissed in his ears. A soft tingle of bubbles rose up his skin as air escaped from his clothing. He felt as weightless as he had in the sky; only his surroundings were changed. When he opened his eyes the salt in the water stung them and he closed them again quickly.

Then something nudged him, a solid form with a wonderfully comforting shape.

The dolphin pressed itself against Connla's body and rose to the surface, lifting him with it. As soon as his head broke free, Connla gulped at the air. Now it seemed precious; now it seemed he could never get enough.

The dolphins cruised very close to him, keeping him afloat with their clustered mass. They could not do so for long and he knew it, but he was grateful for the effort they made. "Are you . . . the one who spoke to me . . .?" he panted to the nearest creature.

"I am."

"Thank you for warning us about the storm, then."

"My warning did you little good," the dolphin observed. "You can do yourself some good, however, if you kick with your legs and swim on your own."

Connla did as he was told, though he had never tried swimming before. The salty water, though cold, had a certain degree of buoyancy, and he soon found he could keep his head above water even without a dolphin beneath him, holding him up.

But why should he? he wondered. Would he not drown soon enough, anyway? Why prolong the agony?

As if it had heard his thoughts, the dolphin said, "You love life, that is why you sought to flee from death to a place where there is no death. If you love life, you must keep worshipping the god of life with your body, which means you must fight to stay alive even when it looks hopeless. Give up, and life will turn its back on you."

Connla managed a quick glance sideways and saw the dolphin with its perpetual toothy grin swimming next to him, its eye bright with old wisdoms.

He gulped another lungful of air and resolved to keep on swimming as long as he could.

A shadow passed over head. The dolphin made a sound Connla could not interpret and suddenly dived, leaving him alone. All the dolphins disappeared at once, in fact. Connla felt a dreadful sense of abandonment and in that moment he might have stopped swimming . . . but he did not. He kicked hard and took another strong stroke with his arms—his body was learning how to swim out of instinct now—and Blathine's voice called down to him, "Reach up so I can catch hold of you."

The horse was no more than a spear's length above Connla, its hooves treading the air just above his head.

He reached up, though the move nearly caused him to sink beneath the surface. At once he felt a strong hand close on his wrist and begin to lift him. He could not believe the slender girl was capable of such strength, yet Blathine drew him up without apparent effort until he was able to swing one leg across the horse's back.

Settled behind her again, he clutched her with all his might. He could feel his heart racing violently. "Where did you go? After I fell off I could not see you anywhere. I thought I would drown."

"But you did not."

"I did not," he agreed, surprised to find himself still alive to say it. "But I do not understand what happened."

Blathine glanced over her shoulder and he saw that she was laughing. He felt a flare of anger; how dare she be amused when he was almost killed!

"Before you came away with me, things happened every day of your life, which you did not understand." she said. "The sun rose but you never knew why, or how, or where it came from, did you?"

"I did not," he admitted.

"Your hair grew and your skin flaked off in tiny particles for no reason you could see," she went on. "When you put enough heated stones into water, it bubbled and you could cook meat in it. Do you know exactly what was happening to make that process take place?"

"I—I do not."

"Every day you saw birds fly in the air without falling, but you never thought that remarkable. Yet you have just had a little experience different from your usual adventures and you are upset; I feel fear in you because you do not understand. Were you ever afraid when you saw one of those birds fly above you, Connla?"

She made him feel foolish. He bit his lip and said nothing.

"Go through life with a merry heart," Blathine advised, "and do not frighten yourself unnecessarily. You fell off the horse, you fell into the sea, and I came back and got you."

"But so much more happened!"

He heard laughter again in her voice. "Did it?"

The horse galloped on.

Five

A<small>T USNA</small>, <small>CONN</small> of the Hundred Battles was distraught over the disappearance of his son. He sent men to the far reaches of his territory and even into enemy lands, asking if anyone had seen Connla. As a reward to the man who found him, Hundred Battles promised to give ten tens of cattle or twelve healthy bondwomen, but his offer had no takers.

Which was just as well, his druid pointed out, because he could not have afforded either reward.

"You are a great trial to me," the old chieftain told Coran. "A man who puts his faith in druids rather than the strength of his own arm is a fool. I listened to you and look what happened. The son on whom my hopes were fastened is gone, and my first wife is lost to me as well."

"She had turned waspish," Coran reminded him.

Now that she was gone, however, Hundred Battles did not remember her that way. When he thought of his first wife, he saw her as the laughing girl he had married, with auburn hair and eyes as blue as the deep summer sky. The more he thought about her, the more precious she seemed to him and the angrier he became with his druid.

"I should never have let you talk me into sacrificing my wife!"

"If her spirit had not been released, who would there be to protect your son now, wherever he is?"

"He would be here with me, where he belongs—and his mother would be here too!" Conn roared, doubling his fists until the knuckles were white.

Grief overcame him. He pushed his food aside and did not look at his other wives. He began pacing the perimeter of his fort and muttering darkly so that his people whispered about his sanity. Young Fiery Hair had gone mad and been seen talking to empty air, they reminded one another. Perhaps the same malady had overtaken his father. In that event, no matter how great the old man's past accomplishments, his clan must face the inevitable and choose a new leader at once.

But Conn of the Hundred Battles had not gone entirely to rust. For a long time, since the land failed, he had feared that very eventuality, and to prepare for it, he had made careful plans. He knew the tribe would not replace him during the height of a war season, so now, to save his office, he declared war against his neighbors to the west and drove out boldly in his chariot to attack them.

"This is a battle my son should be fighting," he said to his charioteer. "But I am still strong; we will prevail."

The charioteer had kissed his one wife goodbye that morning with a heavy heart, never expecting to see her again in this life. He turned a gloomy face toward Hundred Battles. "I hope you are right," he said.

Two lines of chariot warriors came together with a great clash on the Plain of the Stone Men. In the forefront, Conn of the Hundred Battles was dressed in all his chieftainly attire, his crimson battle apron, his heavy gold torc, his boiled leather tunic. Spears that were cast at him bounced harmlessly off that tunic. It would take a mighty sword slash to part such armor, and only a heavy stone could dent the polished bronze helmet protecting the chieftain's skull. He looked every bit a warrior, and his yell was as defiant as if he had seen only two tens of winters.

His opponent was Daire of the Swift Horses, a man not without his own fame as a fighter. Daire's chariot was gaudy with dyed plumes and he had a sizable force of fighting men with him, each anxious to claim the hand that brought down the fabled Conn of the Hundred Battles.

The first rank of men hurled their casting spears, then trotted forward, pulling their iron swords from leather scabbards. As they came together, the chariots wheeled onto a separate battle area and the charioteers began handing their lords' weapons to them—spears and javelins and killing-balls made of great round stones. Scythes were fitted to the spokes of the chariot wheels. This was a battle for blood.

The war trumpets sounded; the warriors roared in an effort to intimidate each other with their ferocity. A bland sun shone down from a cloudless sky, and somewhere in the tall grass small shrews and field creatures went about their own business as on any other day.

Besides all his polished battle skills, Old Hundred Battles had another weapon to bring to the fray. His anger at the loss of his son translated itself into strength for his arm, and when he attacked Daire in one-on-one combat he fought as he had in the old days. Daire, surprised, was forced to fall back.

Conn pursued him with as much righteous rage as if Daire himself were guilty of Connla's abduction. He whirled his chariot in tight to Daire's and heard the satisfying sound of his blades cutting through his enemy's wooden spokes. One side of Daire's chariot dropped suddenly, and the rival chieftain grabbed for the rim, occupying both hands in his instinctive clutch for safety.

At that moment, Conn of the Hundred Battles leaned from his own chariot and delivered the killing blow.

He drove back to Usna in victory, with the head of Daire tied to his chariot. It had been a great victory. His people turned out to line the chariotway and cheer him, to throw flowers and sweet grass at him, to run out with olive wood cups for his men to drink from and wreaths to put around their necks.

"This was like old times," announced Conn's charioteer, surprised and pleased to find himself still alive at the end of the day.

There was no more talk of electing a new chieftain to replace Hundred Battles. And, as if the killing of Daire had offered some undreamt sacrifice to the gods, things began to get better at Usna. The land started producing again. Cows fattened on the grass. The sun shone, birders filled their nets, the streams boiled with fish. A thin layer of fat crept over the people, making their skins glossy and their eyes bright.

The credit, of course, went to Conn of the Hundred Battles.

He sat in his fort, luxuriating in the restoration of his reputation. But in the dark of night, after the candles were extinguished and everyone else was snoring, he lay on his bed and thought of his oldest son.

And sometimes in the darkness, he wept.

၄ာ

He did not know that his beloved son was still in some timeless place, wrapped in enchantment, galloping through corridors of cloud and color on a magical horse. At Usna, existence was neatly divided by light and dark, day and night. In the realm Connla had now entered, all divisions were amorphous and nothing was certain. He and Blathine might have been traveling for a day or a year or a decade; he had no way of knowing.

Yet he never felt hunger, for when his stomach reminded him of his mortality all he had to do was take a bite of the apple Blathine had given him.

When he needed sleep he took it with his head resting on her shoulder. The fairy woman did not seem to sleep at all, nor did Connla ever notice her eating. Yet her eye was ever bright and her energy undiminished.

At last she did say, however, that they should pause long enough to refresh the horse. "When next we stop, we will have reached the Isles of the Blest," she promised. "I would not want to arrive on an ill-treated mount."

Connla had begun to be wary of the earth below. Each time they descended, something upsetting seemed to happen. So he clutched Blathine's waist tightly as they galloped lower, and it was with a distinct feeling of relief that he saw a placid little island appear beneath them, possessing nothing more ominous than a grassy meadow and a clear pool of water.

The horse landed lightfooted beside the pool and lowered its head to drink. "We might as well dismount and move around ourselves," Blathine remarked, putting action to word.

Connla joined her. The horse was drinking in great noisy gulps, and suddenly he found himself wondering how long it had been since he tasted water. He was not thirsty, but the horse's obvious enjoyment tempted him. He bent down beside the pool and cupped his hands to scoop some water into his mouth—and in that moment the apple rolled from his tunic and fell into the water.

He grabbed for it, but too late. It disappeared at once. He reached the full length of his arm into the water and felt around, but could not find the apple. Somewhat alarmed at having lost Blathine's wonderful gift, he waded into the water and crouched down to search the muddy bottom, but still he could not find it.

When at last he was forced to admit defeat and come out of the pool, Blathine was standing on the bank waiting for him. "What will you eat now?" she asked.

At that exact moment his belly cramped with a sudden, furious hunger.

"Have you no food with you?" he asked the fairy woman.

She smiled. "I do not require it as you do."

"But I'm hungry!"

"Yes," she agreed. "You are." Yet she made no effort to help him. All she said was, "It is still a good gallop to the Isles of the Blest and you may die of starvation before we arrive if you don't eat something."

For the first time he noticed that her eyes were not always as clear and limpid as a spring fed pool. Now they seemed opaque; almost cruel. He understood. This was a test she was giving him, like the other incidents.

What might happen if he failed any of the tests, he could not imagine.

He began casting about the tiny island in search of something to eat. There were no trees, and therefore no fruit, no nuts. He crouched and dug in the earth with his fingers but could find no edible roots. No mushrooms hid in the grass. The horse had begun cropping the grass with the same pleasure it had shown on drinking the water, but Connla was not yet hungry enough to imagine eating grass himself.

Then he saw the hare.

It was wiry and brown, just a quick shape leaping at the edge of his vision. At first he could not be certain he had seen it at all, but then it jumped up again and he recognized the animal as real, flesh and blood, edible.

But he had no weapons for hunting a hare.

And in truth, he did not relish the idea of hunting. It was another form of killing, and during the time he had fed on Blathine's apple he had lost some of his taste for meat, for taking nourishment from other warmblooded creatures like himself.

His belly cramped furiously, demanding.

Blathine watched him with an impassive face.

Connla began searching the island until he found a bit of vine twining up a rock formation, and this he pulled free of the earth, to use for fashioning a snare. There were of course no trees, but he found a few clumps of shrubbery to aid in his construction, and he weighted the whole thing with a stone.

When all was in readiness he hesitated. He did not want to kill. Yet he was growing hungrier all the time. His head began to swim; there was a low roaring in his ears. When he walked, he felt as if his knees might collapse beneath him. He knew for a certainty that whenever Blathine was ready to go, she would leave, and if he were too weak to mount the horse and hang on . . .

In desperation he began hunting the hare.

It took a while to sight it again, but at last he flushed it from the tall grass where it was crouched. Holding his arms wide he tried to scare it toward the snare. The animal ran first one way, then another, sometimes doubling back until Connla was certain it had eluded him. He felt himself growing weaker with almost every heartbeat, but he did not dare give up. He staggered, almost fell, recovered and went on.

And the hare leaped just in front of him.

With a mighty effort he shooed it toward the concealed snare. He heard the weighted branch sing free at the moment the trapped animal shrieked with a tiny, heartrending cry.

The hare was still alive when he reached it. It hung head down, forepaws trembling against its breast, and as Connla came up it rolled its eyes toward him.

In his youth Connla had gone on boar hunts, hurling a heavy javelin into savage wild pigs who would kill him if they could. But this, he realized, was different. Now he had at his mercy a small helpless creature much like himself in its vulnerability; much like the baby the granitic giant had wanted to eat.

He stood frozen, staring at the hare. The animal looked back at him.

Connla had never been so hungry in his life, nor so incapable of action.

He heard Blathine's soft step before he saw her, since he stood with his head bowed, unable to look at the trapped hare. The woman put her hand on his arm and he tingled from her touch.

"You must eat," Blathine told him.

"I know it."

"Everything that lives must take nourishment. Eat the hare, Connla; it will make you strong."

Still he hesitated, looking at her. "Surely you are alive, even if you are not like me, Blathine. And you just said that everything which lives must take nourishment. But you also said you do not require food. How can that be?"

Her laugh floated on the air. "Did I say that? Are you so certain? I tell you now, Fiery Hair: I am famished! Kill the hare quickly and build a fire of driftwood from the edge of the island, so we may have a meal before we go on our way."

If the woman was hungry he had to feed her; he was a warrior, a man, a provider. Connla knew he could not delay any longer while he wrestled with sensitive feel-

ings. So he hit the animal in the head with a stone and ·
skinned it with a knife that Blathine provided from a tiny
scabbard affixed to her girdle.

At no point in the operation did he let himself look at
the eyes of the hare.

When it was ready for cooking and the firewood gathered, the fairy woman merely clapped her hands and a
spark leaped from them to the dry twigs. A blaze leaped
up in a bright twist of flame.

"How do you strike fire without flint?" Connla wanted
to know.

"The sun has no flints," Blathine replied. "Yet each
day it brings fire to warm the earth."

Shaking his head ruefully, Connla said, "I see I will
get no simple answers from you."

"There are no simple answers!" she chortled. "How
quickly you are learning!"

Roasting above the flames, the hare began to smell delicious. Connla's mouth flooded with saliva. He could
hardly wait until the meat was half-cooked before rip-
ping it from the improvised spit he had made out of a
green shrubbery-shoot. With both hands he crammed
the smoking meat into his eager mouth.

Nothing had ever tasted so good. Beside it, his fading
memory of Blathine's apple was bland and boring.

But though he had torn the meat into two portions,
the fairy woman was not eating hers. When his own
hunger was somewhat abated, he realized she was sitting
quietly on the ground with her hands folded in her lap.
The meal lay in front of her, untouched and growing cold.

"Aren't you going to eat? I thought you said you were
hungry."

Blathine shrugged. "Not for hare."

He did not wait, but seized her portion and wolfed it
down as well. Only as he was eating the last few bites,
gnawing the sweet red meat from the bone and cutting

the tendons with his teeth, did he look up and see her watching him.

Her expression was so peculiar it almost froze his throat in the act of swallowing.

Lovely Blathine, delicate, airy Blathine, was mimicking every gesture Connla made. She chewed when he chewed, swallowed when he swallowed, just as if she were eating what he was eating. Yet she ate nothing.

Connla stared at her. She smiled back at him, and her tiny pink tongue emerged to lick her red lips in genuine satisfaction.

"Delicious," she said.

What remained of Connla's appetite mysteriously evaporated.

They left the remains of the hare to feed the insects of the island. The horse, having refreshed itself, came trotting up to them and lowered its neck obediently for Blathine's caress. She swung up onto the animal and held her hand down for Connla, but for just one moment the young man hesitated.

He could not have said why; there are no simple answers.

Then her hand closed on his wrist and she gave the slightest tug and lifted him up behind her. The horse flung itself onto the wind and they were off again, galloping west.

To pass the time as they rode, Connla tried to understand what had been happening. The giant, the dolphin . . . and, most of all, Blathine's expression as she watched him eat. It was almost as if she had fed off his feeding. The memory made him wary and he drew back from her a little. But then the perfume of her hair curled into his nostrils and the warmth of her body spoke to him, and he leaned forward again, surrendering.

In that way they went on until the horse changed the angle of its body and Connla felt it descending.

This time, when he looked below, he saw the land of incomparable beauty spread out beneath him which could only be the Isles of the Blest.

There was something familiar about it, he noticed. Straining his eyes to make out details as they dropped ever lower, he thought he could almost recognize the green and rolling plain. He almost knew the mighty forest, the purple mountains. Their names were not strange; he could shape the syllables with his tongue and in his own language. Surely they would come to him in just a moment.

But before he could speak, Blathine said over her shoulder, "Prepare yourself, my hero. Word of our coming has already reached my people and they have prepared a welcome for you."

Then, Connla saw a blaze of bonfires leap from hilltop to hilltop and he heard the sound of singing rise up to him through the clear air, and the names he thought he remembered were forgotten. He was coming home to a strange land amid strange people and his eyes grew wide with wonder.

The horse cantered down through the last few eddies of air until its hooves made thunder on green turf. By the time it halted, a crowd had gathered at the site.

"Blathine!" someone cried. "Connla of the Fiery Hair!" came another voice. Hands reached up to lift the riders down.

Connla was astonished to hear himself greeted by name. He had thought surely his capacity for astonishment was already exhausted.

But Blathine's people not only knew his name, they seemed to know all about him. He overheard one say something to another about Conn of the Hundred Battles, and caught snatches of yet another conversation concerning Connla's own reluctant successes on the battlefield.

The inhabitants of the new land clustered around him, feeling his arms, murmuring admiration for his hair, fingering the fabric of his tunic. They were not aggressive, merely insistently curious. Every one wanted to touch him in some way, and each time one did, he felt the same tingle he had experienced when Blathine touched him.

The sensation was delicious, like tiny bubbles rising in his blood.

Immersed in the crowd, Connla could get no clear idea of what individuals looked like. Faces seemed to blur and all their voices sounded similar, like Blathine's silvery tinkle. But once they had guided him to a bench at the edge of an immaculately kept lawn and indicated that he was to sit there and make himself comfortable, he had an opportunity to study his new acquaintances.

They were not a tall people. Indeed, heart-high Blathine was the tallest among all the women he saw. Slender and well formed, the fairy folk moved with innate grace. When they walked, they flexed the arches of their feet so strongly that they almost seemed to spring from the earth, as if every step were the movement of some dance. Men and women alike had this characteristic; Connla saw no children.

This began to puzzle him. Ten tens of people had assembled on the lawn to welcome himself and Blathine, and among so many there should have been at least a quarter as many children. But the Isles of the Blest, at his first impression, were peopled only with adults.

Sitting beside him, chatting with her friends, Blathine heard his thought. "If no one dies, we need no children as replacements," she said to Connla.

As always, her ability to read his mind startled him, and for the first time it made him slightly uncomfortable. If she could stroll inside his head at will, he had no privacy at all.

This thought, too, she heard. Smiling, she patted his hand. "You have only to ask me to go away and I will," she said reassuringly.

Preparations were underway for a festival to celebrate Connla's arrival. A number of lovely young women came forward with ropes of flowers, which they used as decorations, swagging them from the branches of trees that stood at the perimeter of the lawn. Birds of a dazzling whiteness fluttered onto these flower ropes and perched there, singing. A gentle breeze rippled across the countryside, setting the leaves to dancing and causing the taller grasses to nod in rhythm. Everything was light-hearted and gay, no cloud darkened the sky, no weed threatened the perfection of the lawn.

No time passed.

Connla sat on his bench and Blathine's people came up to him, introducing themselves. Some had unpronounceable names, others called themselves after birds or flowers or character traits. One such was an endearing little fellow with pointed ears. "I am Whimsical," he told Connla. "But you may just call me "Whim" if you like."

The fairy folk included Connla in their conversation with Blathine, gossiping cheerfully about various things that had happened in her absence, commenting on this or that mutual acquaintance, asking Connla his opinion of their land or their bird music or the clothing they wore.

Indeed, as he had already noticed, their clothing was most strange. A few wore sheer robes similar to Blathine's, but many draped themselves in leaves or mosses and some wore odd, flashing garments that seemed to be plaited moonbeams. For jewelry, they wore not only gold and silver and colored stones, but also seashells and feathers and random bits of spiderweb pearled with unmelting ice. Fairy footgear was just as varied, ranging from barefoot to Blathine's delicate slippers, to great clumping boots of an indeterminate substance too shiny to be leather.

All of this attire was put together in the most artless way so that no two people were dressed alike and each costume seemed to reflect its wearer's distinct personality.

Connla began to feel very badly dressed, with nothing but a nondescript tunic to cover his body.

No sooner had this thought occurred to him than his new friend Whimsical came trotting up with a great cloak spread over his two arms, a piece of glowing fabric the exact color of new copper. "This is for you!" Whimsical announced with a delighted grin.

Standing up, Connla draped the cloak around his shoulders. The material was unlike any he had ever seen. Warm to the touch as if heated from within, it seemed to ripple against his hands like an animal seeking to be caressed. But if he closed his fist upon it, it pulled away of its own accord, refusing to be treated roughly. As soon as the cloak settled around him he felt taller, broader, safer, more sure of himself . . . and also more sensitive, more aware of every nuance in the atmosphere around him.

Blathine nodded approvingly. "The cloak becomes you," she said.

He stroked it—gently. "This should be warm on the coldest days."

"Coldest days? We have no cold days here!"

"Do you mean it is always summer?"

She shrugged. "Not summer, not winter, not spring, not autumn. We have no need for seasons, as we do not plant."

Connla glanced at the sky, lit with the same unvarying light he had observed since first arriving. "Doesn't it even get cooler at night?"

"No night. Since we do not sleep, we do not need darkness."

She had indicated this before, but now the full weight of its meaning began to dawn upon him. "Do you mean it's just like this, *all the time?*"

"Of course," Blathine replied. "In the Isles of the Blest the sky is always blue and cloudless and the light is always strong enough to cast shadows, but never so strong it hurts the eyes."

"And you do not eat or drink . . ."

"Ah, some of us do. In some ways. Like butterflies sipping nectar, some of us have requirements," Blathine told him.

"What of me, what will I eat here?"

"We will get another apple for you. You will never be hungry or thirsty."

Connla remembered the earlier apple; then he remembered the incredibly delicious taste of the roasted hare he had eaten on the island of grass. True, he had had to kill the animal—but how good it had been! How crisp and crackling the golden-brown skin, how sweet and gamy the firm flesh! Was he never to eat a hare again? Or roast pork from a well-hunted boar? Or cold buttermilk in an olivewood goblet, or golden mead brewed from fragrant honey . . .?

A sense of loss washed over him.

Six

BLATHINE PRESSED CLOSE. Her breath was as fragrant as honey-mead; her warmth was like the warmth of summer. "You have lost nothing of value, Connla," she whispered, "by comparison with what we offer you here."

Looking down into her eyes he found himself believing her and his depression lifted. She was beautiful; she was his. He now lived in a land without death and pain, in a place where no one need ever go hungry or fear the dark—or be sacrificed in a wicker basket to cruel and indifferent gods.

Connla of the Fiery Hair was a brave man. His distaste for battle had not been due to a lack of courage, and now he demonstrated that courage by taking a deep breath and plunging fully into his new life as if leaping into a cold lake.

"I accept all you have to offer, Blathine," he told the fairy woman. "And gladly! You will see no more sadness in my face and hear no complaints from my lips. Do I see a set of dancers forming over there? Come, let us join them and dance together!" He grabbed her hands and tugged her toward the group.

With a merry laugh Blathine joined him. "We will dance," she said. "And never get tired!"

So they danced and laughed and Connla was introduced to more inhabitants of the Isles of the Blest, some of whom had come across a narrow stretch of water from a nearby island belonging to the same realm. Their little boat was drawn up on the shore, bedecked with flowers and sporting a painted sail. "When we have danced all the dances anyone knows," they told Connla, "you must come with us to our island and see how lovely it is. This one shines, but ours sparkles!"

Some of those who lived on Blathine's island frowned when they heard this. "Your land is no more comely than ours," they argued.

"It is!"

"It is not!"

A third group injected itself into the discussion at that point. "Our island is more fair than either of these," said a hawkish man with lavender-colored eyes. "I grow tired of hearing these claims of superiority, when everyone knows my place is best."

Now there were three groups glowering at each other. Connla was puzzled. Turning to Blathine, he inquired, "How many Isles of the Blest are there?"

"No one has ever been able to count them. Sometimes it appears as if just one land rises from the sea; sometimes the surface of the ocean is speckled with them like freckles on a sun-kissed face. They are all one land, really, joined by the connecting web of fairy power. My people are the Sidhe—you pronounce it *Shee* in your coarse tongue—and very strong, you know. Everything concerning us is gilded with enchantment to disguise and protect us from the eyes of mortals. So even our lands are a puzzlement."

Connla scratched his head. "Even to yourselves?"

She was laughing at him. "Of course!"

She was in a good mood but it was obvious her friends were not. The argument had grown hotter. Some men were knotting their fists and others were muttering in threatening undertones.

The foolishness of the burgeoning quarrel was apparent to Connla, and he stepped forward to try to stop it. "Why should you be angry over such a trifle? I am certain all your islands are beautiful, especially if, as Blathine tells me, they are really just parts of one land. You are friends and brothers and countrymen; there is no need for one to claim superiority over another."

The hawkish man favored Connla with an icy glare from his lavender-colored eyes. "You are a fool," he said. Between one heartbeat and the next, a knife materialized in his hand, a strange glowing weapon with a jeweled hilt and a rippled blade.

Connla sucked in air, and his belly—moving back from the menace of the knife. The hawkish man advanced immediately, making patterns in the air with the point of his blade.

"This is not my fight," Connla protested.

"Of course it is," the other replied. "You are a warrior, are you not? Welcome to war!" So saying, he leaped at Connla.

As if this had been a signal, the crowd exploded into battle. Every fairy man seemed to have had a weapon hidden about him somewhere, and now they attacked each other with wild impartiality, arms swinging, fists clubbing, knives and swords and spears doing deadly work. Connla was so taken aback, he could not at first even defend himself. Of all the unexpected things which had happened since he came away with Blathine, this was the most surprising to him.

These people obviously meant to kill him. In spite of all the things the fairy woman had said about the Isles of the Blest.

With all his heart, Connla wished he had stayed home.

Something pressed against him for just a heartbeat, something as intangible as a memory. Above the rising tumult he thought he heard a voice. It was not Blathine's silvery voice, yet it was somehow familiar. This one was phlegmy and tired . . . it almost reminded the young man of his mother's voice. *Fight*, it sighed. *And fear nothing. You have thrown away the blessing of death.*

At those words a heat ran through Connla, like the re-membered heat emanating from a wicker basket atop a faraway, long ago hill. He ran forward to meet the laven-der-eyed man. He had no weapon, but snatched one from someone else in passing. A short sword, it was, of a de-sign he did not know but with a satisfying balance and a good weight to the hilt. Protecting himself, he drove the sword straight at the fairy man who had attacked him, and saw blood spurt.

The lovely lawn became a scene of carnage.

No matter how hard Connla fought, there always seemed to be more angry men coming at him. He fell back, gulped frantic lungfuls of air and returned to the fray, trying to catch a glimpse of Blathine somewhere beyond the lunging bodies and bobbing heads. More than anything else, he wanted an explanation. If he was going to die, he at least wanted to confront her first and have her admit her lies and trickery.

The fighting grew more intense. Like all battles, it de-veloped a rhythm of its own—thrust and parry, advance and fall back—which Connla knew and understood. He found himself shoulder to shoulder with fairy men who seemed to be on the same side he was, and who laughed aloud with the joy of battle. He was not accustomed to thinking of battle as fun, but it seemed that these men did. Their attitude began to infect him. When he struck a particularly good blow and his companions cheered him, Connla found himself smiling and feeling proud, accepting a wink of congratulation with unexpected pleasure.

No time passed.

The fight went on and on. Men bled and died and were trampled, but Connla managed to stay on his feet, though he had received several wounds. If he was still alive when the battle was over, he knew those wounds would hurt. But in the excitement of the moment they caused him no pain; their only effect was to make him anxious for reprisals.

When he next drew away from the center of the conflict to catch his breath and wipe the sweat from his eyes, he noticed that very few men were left standing. Not enough to conduct a decent battle at all, really. And those few survivors had begun to swing their weapons in a most desultory fashion, as if any real interest in the war had gone out of them and they were merely going through the final motions of an insignificant ritual.

It occurred to Connla that no one would notice if he just walked away.

Then a deep bellow of sound roared out upon the air, swelling to fill it, crowding out the noise of metal striking metal and the grunts of men hitting men. A man wrapped in a cloak of spotted fur strode into the center of the battle area, holding a huge curved shell to his lips. When he blew upon the shell, the sound trumpeted forth again and the remaining fighters thrust their weapons through their belts and stepped back from one another.

"The battle is over," announced the shell-player.

A lighthearted mood took hold of the survivors. As if their fellows were not lying bleeding and dead at their feet, they began chattering to one another, laughing, gesticulating, carrying on as if nothing had happened. Connla could hardly believe his eyes.

Blathine came up to him. "Did you enjoy the battle?" she wanted to know.

"I have never enjoyed battle. I do not like killing others, it makes me sad. Such a waste . . ." He held out his hands, palms open, trying to communicate his feeling to her.

But, for once, Blathine did not seem able to read his mind at all. "You are being ridiculous," she told him. "Why get upset about something of no importance? You just had a good time, did you not, using your strength and skills and seeing how good you were? Come, now it is time to enjoy something else." She caught him by the elbow in a grip of astonishing strength and steered him away from the scene of the battle. But he looked over his shoulder at the dead, and in his heart Connla wept.

"This was not my fight," he said to them softly. "I did not want to harm any of you."

He could not understand how the war had happened.

He wanted to take time to salute his slain enemies for the valiant warriors they had been.

He wanted time to grieve for them as was proper, though he had not known them personally.

But he was carried away from them on a cresting wave of fairy folk, who were as happy and festive as if nothing had happened.

Connla felt a growing anger. Blathine had tricked him with her lies and promises, bringing him to a strange place he could not hope to understand, to live among callous people whom he could never learn to like. Even her radiant beauty seemed to dim as he thought of the way she had fooled him. He tried to pull his arm away from her.

"Be careful of your wounds!" she said, with that shimmery laugh of hers, as if wounds were a mere joke.

He paused to consider his wounds, the knife thrust he had taken to his ribs, the chop of a sword against his shoulder, the slam of a stone against his skull. But, to his surprise, he still felt no pain. He pulled aside his coppery cloak then, and studied his body intently.

There was no blood showing. No cut, no bruise, no abrasion anywhere.

When he raised his fingers to feel his head, he found no bump.

Blathine was laughing very hard. "Have you already forgotten what I told you? Look back!" She turned and waved her arm toward the scene of the recent battle.

No corpses littered the earth. Men unmarked by blood were getting to their feet, shaking themselves off. A few bent over to collect severed limbs or fingers. As Connla stared with a gaping mouth, they held these parts against their severed flesh and the members reattached themselves, new skin quickly spreading to cover the jointure. Within a few breaths' time, men who should have been dead were whole again and coming to join the festival.

One in particular met Connla's eyes and headed straight for him—his first victim, the hawkish man. He was grinning broadly. A faint rust-colored stain was just fading from the front of his tunic, where Connla's sword had delivered its killing thrust.

"Well fought, mortal man!" he said, clapping Connla on the shoulder. "I like you. We shall have much fun together, you and I. When next we fight I will kill you, I think, for I am actually much better at fighting than you are. But it was only simple hospitality to let a new arrival win the first time.

"Oh, by the way," he added as an afterthought, while Connla stared at him, speechless with shock. "My name is Fiachna and I am a Master of the Blue Sword. I will teach you something of my art if you like, so we will be more evenly matched." So saying, he turned away and a

beautiful fairy woman ran into his open arms, smiling up
at him. "Sweet wife," Fiachna murmured, bending his
head to hers. The couple strolled away with their arms
around each other's waists.

"He is . . . not . . . dead," Connla said very carefully,
as if each word were a stone almost too heavy for him to
lift. "I did not . . . kill him. Or anyone. Yet I struck killing blows."

"You did," Blathine agreed. "If Fiachna teaches you
the secrets of the Blue Sword, you will be a fighter almost
without equal."

"But why aren't they dead?"

She answered him with the gentle exasperation of a
mother whose child refuses to learn a simple lesson. "We
do not suffer. We do not die. We do not quarrel in real
anger, but only enough to incite a battle which everyone
enjoys. Our menfolk get to demonstrate their grace and
artistry with weapons and we women cheer them on.
When the battle is over, all are restored to fight again, of
course—whenever the mood takes them and they find
pleasure in it."

Her eyes were twinkling. "But there are other pleasures, my Fiery Hair. You have had a lovely battle; now
come with me to my bower and experience some of the
other delights my kingdom has to offer."

Dazed, Connla let her lead him as she liked.

They encountered other men and women of the fairy
folk, also walking very close together, gazing fondly at
one another. All seemed headed in the same direction, a
cluster of lacy spires and domes which, upon closer in-
spection, proved to be pergolas fashioned of precious
metal and surrounded by scented hedges. Each pergola
formed a small, private chamber, open to the sweet air
but closed off from the curious eyes of passersby.

Blathine led Connla to one of the most beautiful of
these outdoor rooms, a bower entwined with vines of

some trumpet-shaped purple flower that added its own heady perfume to the scented air. A tiny gate swung open at her touch; birds sang an invisible welcome from the shrubbery.

"Welcome to my home," Blathine said.

Connla looked around. There was no furniture, no solidity to the leafy walls, no roof. For all its dainty charm, this bower could hardly be called a dwelling place. "But where do you really live?" he could not resist asking.

"Here. Or there. Anywhere I like."

"Outside always? What protects you from . . ." Then he stopped himself. He had almost said, "What protects you from the weather?" before he realized she would laugh at him again. Had she not already explained? There was no inclement weather on the Isles of the Blest.

Connla struggled to learn faster. "What protects you from the grass when you—when we—lie down? Is there no dew?"

His reference to "we" made Blathine's lips curve in a smile of incredible sweetness. "Your cloak will make a bed for us," she said. "There is indeed dew. When you feel the need of its particular type of refreshment, just gather enough to wash your face, and all the little lines and sags of mortal flesh will be rinsed away. But for now, do not think of such things. Do not think of anything but me, Connla." She tilted her face up toward his and he saw the delicate sheen of her eyelids, moist with youth; the curve of her perfect lashes; the invitation of her soft lips.

The coppery cloak was flung on the earth in a heartbeat, and in another heartbeat Blathine was in Connla's arms.

How yielding her flesh was! As tender and firm as mortal flesh, it gave itself freely to his touch, letting him explore the fairy-form with growing wonder. For Blathine was not quite like a mortal woman. Even as he touched her shoulder or her breast she somehow looked into his mind and saw exactly how he liked that portion of a woman to be, and shaped herself to suit him. So his hands created perfection, according to his own standard and desire, and when he had caressed her entire body other women were ruined for him forever. None could hope to equal what Blathine had become, to please him.

She said a thousand flattering things to Connla, indicating that he was as perfect for her as she for him. Whatever he wanted to ask of her, she gave before he could ask it, and whatever he did, she delighted in.

Within the bower of Blathine, Connla discovered the true enchantment of the Sidhe.

No time passed.

He was tireless. She was radiant. The boundaries that separate men and women in daily life dissolved between them, and they lay with their hearts touching in spirit as well as in truth. *For this*, Connla thought, *I gladly leave Erin and Hundred Battles and all the worries and sorrows of that life. For this I gladly leave life itself. Let me dwell forever*, he implored whatever gods might be listening, *in this mist of glamour.*

Around them, birds were weaving wreaths of music so tender Connla held his breath to listen. Blathine lay quietly in his arms, with her eyes closed, and he wondered if she was asleep. Then he remembered her telling him that her people did not sleep. Yet, when he looked at her, the rise and fall of her breast was so calm, her eyes so still beneath their glossy lids, he felt certain she slumbered.

Could this mean that other things she had told him were also untrue? Or could this merely be another instance of his misunderstanding? So many things in the realm of the fairy folk defied his understanding.

He knew only that he was happy. He had found a paradise. In the Isles of the Blest there really was no suffering, at least not in any permanent sense; even warfare was merely a game in which men might battle as much as they liked, secure in the knowledge that there would always be another battle.

Connla rolled over onto his back and his coppery cloak snuggled around him, fitting itself to his form and making him even more comfortable. Folding his arms behind his head, the young man stared up at the sky. The serene, cerulean sky.

Which would always be serene. Would always be blue.

Always. Always.

Seven

BLATHINE OPENED HER eyes. "Were you sleeping?" he asked her.

She smiled. What a bewitching curve her lips had! "Of course not. But we do rest sometimes, just to give ourselves the pleasure of contrast between quietness and activity. Do you feel a need to sleep?"

He considered this. "I do not. I feel wonderful." He was surprised to find this was true. He had made a long journey, fought a desperate battle, loved a beautiful . . . creature, and yet he felt as fresh as if he had just arisen on a spring morning.

Suddenly Blathine sprang to her feet, holding out her hand to encourage him to join her. "Let me show you more of your new home," she invited.

Hand in hand the two of them explored the far reaches of the realm. In wonder, Connla saw azure mountains rise from broad plains where there had been no mountains when last he looked. Trees appeared, budded, blossomed. Landscape shifted; changed. When they required a pathway, the grass lay down before the couple, offering them smooth footing. When they climbed a hill, it seemed to tilt beneath them so that no effort was required to ascend—it was as easy as walking on level land. Yet when they got to the top, they saw marvelous views in all directions.

No sooner did Connla think of picking an armful of flowers to give to Blathine, than a veritable garden bloomed beside them. Connla had only to turn and reach to select an array of gorgeous blooms.

The young man was curious to know just what plants thrived in the fairy kingdom, so he waded in among the flowers and bent to examine individual ones. Blathine followed him.

"That is foxglove," she pointed out. "The blossoms are the right size to glove the hands of the smallest of my people. And there you see harebell, and primroses that make the invisible visible. Do not tread on them, they are valuable!

"The cowslips over here are called the key to gold, Connla. They mark the places where we have buried our treasure. And oh, see the beautiful violas and the bluebells! These are my favorites, I think.

"And just look up—do you see that low hill? With wild thyme growing upon it? In your land, a hill like that would be a fairy mound, and if one of the mortals gathered the tops of the thyme and made a tea of them and drank it, he could see us at our revels."

"Does every plant and flower have special properties?" Connla asked.

The fairy woman nodded. "They do. Each thing that lives has its purpose. Your druids know something of this, my love."

With an effort, his mind reaching back to a fading memory, Connla recalled his father's chief druid, Coran. The man who had burnt his mother.

"What a dreadful scowl is on your face!" Blathine said.

"I was thinking of the druid I know best, an evil man. He sacrificed my mother in a wicker basket, in an effort to keep me from you."

"He is a wicked man indeed," Blathine agreed. "I told you, we have no use for druids here." Her voice dripped contempt like a corrosive acid.

Blathine, Connla thought to himself, was a bundle of contradictions. "Yet you spoke of them with respect just now," he reminded her. "You said they know something of your wisdom."

Her eyes were hard as anthracite, and deep within them sullen fires glowed. "And how do you think the druids acquired that knowledge, foolish mortal? They stole it from us!"

"From the Sidhe?"

"So it was. In the youth of your race we moved freely among your people, letting them see us, enjoying their company. There seemed no harm in them, not at first. They had the clear eyes of animals or children and had no difficulty observing all we did. Then they began copying us. At first it was just our herbalism they employed, and some of them showed quite a gift for it. Not as good as we could do, of course," she added with a sniff of pride, "but they did learn how to heal simpler illnesses and less-than-deadly wounds. Not content with that, however—for mortals have never learned how to be content—they began to attempt our more complex rituals. Some showed talents for these as well. There were men of your people who could change the weather almost as well as we could, and others who could work various enchantments on their fellows.

"All this they learned from watching us. But they had no restraint, no temperance. They soon moved past employing fairy arts to make life more pleasant, and began using those arts to gain advantage over one another. They started doing dangerous things with magic, using its power in ways that made the gods shudder. Power is neither good nor evil, Connla; it just *is*. The good or evil comes from the way it is employed.

"I will speak frankly. The way mortals began using the magic they had learned from our people frightened us. We could foresee great harm being done, and we did not want the responsibility for it. The Sidhe dislike responsibility. We find its weight crushing and so we avoid it, as mortals avoid carrying great boulders around on their backs.

"When mortals organized themselves into priesthoods we began avoiding them. We were confident our magic was still more powerful, but we felt robbed and we were angry. Weaving spells we had not shown to your kind, we made ourselves invisible to mortal eyes except on occasions of our choosing. And we gave them no further bits of knowledge they could misuse.

"But we acted too late, I fear. Those who called themselves druids, your most gifted users of arcane arts, continued to develop their abilities on their own. From generation to generation they passed down the wisdoms and the rituals they remembered from the time when human and fairy shared the earth in friendship.

"Now they turn those very spells against us. They try to keep us from our normal pursuits. They even search for ways to find our hidden gold and steal it, as if stolen knowledge were not enough. But then, as I said, mortals are never content with what they have."

Blathine gave her delicate shoulders a tiny shrug. "This is a very unpleasant subject and I do not like unpleasant subjects. If I were not so fond of you, my Fiery Hair, I would not have spoken of it at all. Let us do something bright and gay instead!" She gave a tinkling laugh like the chiming of some tiny bell and skittered away from him.

Connla ran after her. "Wait!"

But she moved so quickly he could not catch up. No matter how hard he ran, the fairy woman effortlessly outpaced him. She glanced back over her shoulder, laughing and mocking him.

Their race drew the attention of other fairy folk, who soon joined in, shouting encouragement to one another. Soon, a whole ribbon of them was weaving over the undulating green hills, dancing amid the flowers, skipping over burbling brooks and bounding over butterflies. Every one of them could run faster than Connla and jump higher, and he began to grow suspicious.

"You are using magic to beat me!" he called out to Blathine.

She checked her pace enough to allow him to almost catch up. "Of course I am," she replied. "Magic is one-seventh of what I am."

Connla had never heard of fractions. "What is the rest of you?" he panted.

"Air," she told him over her shoulder. "And water. Fire and folly. Art and imagination." Then she showed him her silver heels and ran completely away from him.

The troop of the Sidhe sped after her, Connla in the rear and striving mightily not to be left behind altogether.

The hawkish-looking man whom he had fought and killed dropped back to run beside him.

"Fiachna, is it?"

The other nodded. "I am called Fiachna, when it suits me. No one should have to bear the same name forever; it would become too stale on the tongue. You will be known by other names yourself, Connla Fiery Hair."

This was hard for Connla to imagine. "I like the name I have."

"Happy for you, then. But when Blathine wants to be someone else you will have to change too, or be left behind."

Connla frowned. "She won't leave me, she loves me."

Fiachna stopped in his tracks and gave the human man a long look from beneath peaked eyebrows. "Love? What has love to do with us? We are the Sidhe."

"I do not understand."

"Love implies responsibility, Connla. Both are human things; we avoid them. Pain and loss, worry and obligation—they have no place in the Isles of the Blest."

It had never occurred to Connla that Blathine might not love him as he loved her. He knew he loved her; he could feel the emotion curled up inside his chest, warm and delicious. And she had gone to much trouble to win him and bring him back with her. That must mean that she felt the same.

When he said this to Fiachna the fairy man laughed. "You have a lot to learn. She wanted you, which is not the same thing as love at all."

"You may possess the wisdom of the Sidhe," Connla answered hotly, "but in this instance you are wrong. I know Blathine loves me."

"Ask her, then," Fiachna suggested.

"I will." *I will ask her*, Connla repeated silently to himself. *I will do it as soon as I have the opportunity, though I know I do not have to fear her answer.*

So confident was he, he was in no hurry to ask the question. He was only in a hurry to catch up with Blathine.

"Tell me this, Fiachna, since you know so much. Can you make me run faster so I may keep up with my lady?"

Fiachna nodded. "Nothing simpler. Mind your heels." So saying, he waved both his thumbs at Connla's feet and at once the young man felt himself spurt forward, as if propelled by a mighty wind.

He had never run so fast. When he put foot to earth he snatched it off quicker than thought and had taken three more steps before he realized it. He left Fiachna behind; he cut through the troop of the Sidhe like a sharp knife through stale bread; he came abreast of Blathine in a twinkling and called out to her joyfully.

"How nice to see you again!" she told him with a bright smile.

"Where are we running to?" he asked.

"Running to? We are not running *to* anything, we are running for the pleasure of running. And now we will stop, for the pleasure of stopping."

And so she did, and the rest of the troop with her. But Connla could not stop.

Dismayed, he ran right past Blathine and sped onward. His mind told his feet to slow down but they would not obey. They would churn the earth, they would leap the air, but they would not stop and stand still.

"Wait!" Blathine cried. "Are you not going to stay here with me?"

"I would if I could," Connla called back to her ruefully. "But my feet have their own mind about it. Fiachna put an enchantment on them and they are running away with me. Undo the enchantment for me, beloved."

Something that might almost have been a frown— except that she never really frowned—crossed Blathine's face, like the faintest shadow of a cloud in a sunlit sky. "I cannot. If one of the Sidhe began undoing the magic of another there would be no end of trouble about it."

With all his strength, Connla was finally managing to force his feet to run in an enormous circle around Blathine so that he could at least talk to her. "But what will happen to me?" he wanted to know. "How am I to stop?"

Her eyes looked sad. "You will have to find your own way to do that." Then she brightened. "But it will mean a grand war. As you are really a guest of our king while in the Isles of the Blest, it is his reputation for hospitality that Fiachna sullies by discomforting you in this way. I will go and tell the king at once, so he can summon warriors to attack Fiachna and punish him."

At her words the fairy men gathered near her broke into a lusty cheer, obviously ready for a new battle.

"But what about *me*?" Connla wailed.

They had already forgotten him. Everyone was scurrying off in search of weapons and fighting comrades. Even Blathine was trotting briskly in a new direction, looking for the king of the Sidhe to tell him of the incident. No one was paying any attention at all to the unfortunate cause of the upcoming hostilities.

Connla let his feet carry him away, wherever they willed. He felt painfully unnecessary, which was a new experience for him.

I might as well continue my tour of the realm of the Sidhe, he thought to himself. At least I will have that pleasure.

His tireless feet carried him at breathtaking speed across the land, however, so he was not able to admire any of it in the detail he wished. He caught brief glimpses of what appeared to be cities, crystal-spired and glittering, lit from within in some mysterious way. Elsewhere, dark forests loomed and he heard the howl of some unknown animal, a sound so chilling it sent shivers down his spine.

Whatever it is, I can outrun it, he reassured himself. *At least there's that consolation. And no one dies here.*

Unless . . . A terrible thought struck him. This was supposed to be an island, or islands, which meant they ended somewhere and the sea began. Was there any chance his feet might carry him off the land and into the sea? His one effort to control them—when he had circled around to speak to Blathine—had been almost beyond his strength. He doubted he could do it again. If his feet chose to take him out into the water, he might drown.

His feet ran on.

Green meadows flashed past. Hills rose, dwindled, fell away. And still he did not come to a seashore. He had not turned but was running in a straight line, so surely he should reach the edge of the island soon.

Yet he ran and ran and there was always more land in front of him. That which had been composed of several islands, or a cluster of islands, or a whole world of islands when he arrived, now seemed to be one endless stretch of land. And every bound was carrying him farther and farther away from Blathine.

The farther he got from her, the more he realized he loved her.

She flooded his memory like moonlight. His nostrils seemed to fill with the fragrance of her, his hands ached to hold hers. His ears yearned for the sound of her voice. She became more precious to him with every step. He forgot to look at the countryside and turned his vision inward, staring at images of Blathine and wondering if he would ever see her again.

Then, another image shoved hers aside—quite rudely, he thought. An elderly woman, fat and with a discontented face, filled his mind. It took him a few heartbeats to recognize her as his dead mother.

"Mother!" he gasped. He could not imagine why she was entering his thoughts at such a time.

My son, she replied, in a voice like a distant echo at the back of a sea cave. She held out her hands beseechingly. *You will do yourself harm if you go on this way for too long. Stop now, I implore you. You are in the land of the Sidhe but you are not one of them; you have a mortal body, even if it cannot die in this place. No man can run endlessly without doing terrible damage to himself. Stop, for my sake.*

"I would if I could," he assured her, feeling foolish for speaking aloud to a voice that was only in his own head. "But my feet are under a spell."

You must stop! she repeated urgently. *Your lungs will fill with blood. The muscles in your legs will tear themselves*

*to shreds. You will eventually become a monster so hideous
that the others will turn their faces away to avoid seeing you.*

Her words frightened him. He was not certain if she
was really there . . . Who could be certain of anything in
this place? But he began to suspect she was there at least
in some sense. And she was trying to protect him.

"Why have you come to warn me?"

Because I love you, she said.

Love.

Blathine had let him run off without warning him at
all.

But Blathine loved him, too. He believed it; he was absolutely certain of it.

Almost.

His mother's face stayed vivid in his mind while his
feet ran on and on. He began to hear his breathing, great
rasping breaths that did not sound right to him. And
there were pains creeping up the backs of his legs, as if
the muscles were beginning to fray from the strain he
was putting upon them. "Can you help me?" he asked
the vision of his mother.

I have no magic but love, she told him.

"Then if that is magic, use it!"

She closed her eyes then, and stretched her arms
wider. A sense of warmth poured over Connla. He forgot
the times he had been as impatient with her as his own
father had often been. He forgot the times she had scolded
him, or neglected him, or made what seemed unreason-
able demands of him. He remembered her only as a source
of comfort and security when he was small, and he longed
for that security again.

My son, her voice whispered softly.

He relaxed into the vision, letting go. Her imagined
arms closed around him. His tense muscles softened; his
taut tendons eased.

His enchanted feet slowed their mad racing, then stopped. Connla stood with his head hanging and his chest heaving, leaning against . . . the wind. When he opened his eyes, his mother was not there. He was alone. Yet the sense of her presence lingered.

He shook himself, hardly daring to believe the frightening experience was over. Hesitantly, he raised one foot and took a step, but the foot made no effort to run away with him again. It was just an obedient foot, under the control of his own mind.

He mopped the sweat from his brow and turned around, to retrace the long way he had come and return at last to Blathine.

Now that he could walk, he could appreciate the countryside in detail. Truly, he had never seen a land so beautiful. He lingered to admire sparkling lakes and crystalline pools and leaping waterfalls. Beside meadows tapestried with wildflowers he paused to give his nostrils a treat, enjoying the numerous perfumes that wafted to him on the warm breeze. The trip became one long delight.

The Isles of the Blest, Connla thought to himself, were truly named. He saw fat deer grazing in lush grass, fearless as if they had no natural enemies. Perhaps they did not, here. Fat little brown animals popped out of holes in the earth and surveyed him as he passed, but they did not seem nervous, either. When he crouched down and held out his hand, one hopped trustingly onto his palm to have a better look at him. It cocked its round little head to one side and met his gaze with liquid eyes. The creature was plump and glossy; meaty.

Yet he felt no appetite for it.

I may never eat meat again, he thought.

Then he remembered the hare he had slain and devoured with such zest. Never eat meat again? Never enjoy that delicious taste, feel good grease running down his chin, crunch bones?

The animal on his palm looked at him with total trust. Gently, Connla set it down upon the earth and went on, musing to himself.

He found himself wandering along the shore of a reed-filled lake. A dark bird with red patches on its wings was perched atop a catkin, singing. Willows crowded the fringe of the lake. A great thirst came upon Connla and he knelt by the water, cupping his hands to scoop up a drink. But as he bent over, a fish with green scales rose to the surface and flicked its tail, sending a spray of water into the young man's face.

He drew back, startled. The fish circled and came toward him, head on. Lifting its snout clear of the water, it announced in a bubbly voice, "This is my place, find your own." Then it submerged with a mighty splash.

So, not only dolphins, but even common fish could speak!

"Everything has some way of communication," a voice commented close by him. He glanced around but saw nothing, neither fish nor animal. He gave the bird with the red wings a suspicious look but it sang on, oblivious to him.

"Who spoke?" he asked.

"We spoke," came the answer.

Connla scrambled to his feet. He felt better meeting the unexpected on his feet.

"Who is 'we'?"

The wind sighed over the water and the reeds stirred in unison. "The water dancers," they murmured, their massed voices a sibilant song.

Even reeds had the gift of speech? Connla rubbed his eyes and knuckled his ears, hoping to clear the cobwebs from his mind. "If you can really speak," he said to the reeds, "why did I never know this before?"

"Very few attempt to talk with us," came the answer. "Some talk to trees, or flowers, but we are considered so common that we are quite ignored."

"I am afraid I have always ignored reeds myself," Connla admitted.

The chorus of reeds hummed in disapproval. *I wonder if they mean to do me some harm*, Connla thought.

"We harm no one," the reeds said.

They were hearing his thoughts, then, as Blathine so often did! He should have realized it sooner. They had more powers and gifts than he had ever suspected. Was this true of all things, perhaps?

Possibilities of wonder sprang from the idea, spreading out before him like concentric rings of unguessed colors.

Overhearing his speculations, the reeds commented, "When you walk in a forest, you are never alone but surrounded by a vast community of trees. Do you not ever feel their presence?"

"Perhaps I have," Connla admitted uncertainly, trying to recall.

"And if you cross a meadow, each time you set down your foot you set it upon a host of living things, grasses and flowers and insects. Have you not sensed this?"

Appalled, Connla took a step back from the verge of the lake. "I have not!" But now that he knew, could he ever walk on grass again?

The massed reeds made a sound like rustling hay, which Connla somehow understood was their way of expressing laughter. "Plants are not harmed by the weight of a quick foot," they told him. "We are resilient; more so than you. It is only the cutting edge that can hurt us"—at this, a shiver ran across the reeds—"or some poison in our water. We ask only that you be aware of us, for we are small and humble things. Do us no intentional unkindnesses. Do not overlook us as if we do not exist, though we are a faceless mass to you."

Having recently been overlooked by the Sidhe as they prepared for the excitement of a war, Connla felt sympathy for the water-grasses. Promising to remember them and the wisdom they had given him, he turned to be on his way.

Then they spoke to him one last time, on a puff of wind that might have blown in from the sea he had not found. "You yourself might be no more than a reed to Something Else," they cautioned.

They fell silent, and try as he might, he could not persuade them to speak to him again.

Resuming his journey, Connla was lost in thought. He looked with fresh eyes at everything he passed, taking comfort in the new knowledge that he was not alone.

Alone. Hardly! He moved through crowds. Birds and butterflies and bugs, every manner of green and leafy thing, kept him company as he traveled. Now that he knew they had the gift of communication, he sent his thoughts to them from time to time, as one might raise a hand in cheery greeting to a stranger on the road. And sometimes a bird sang out a reply, or a butterfly alit on his shoulder, to ride for a while. Or a tree dipped a branch in salute.

In this way he covered much ground.

The sky never changed; day never faded, night never fell. Connla found himself wondering what was happening among the Sidhe in his absence. Had the war already been fought? He felt a twinge of regret, realizing he might have missed it. With the threat of death removed, battle had become a joyous sport and he longed to take part in it again.

Surely the Isles of the Blest, where all wishes seemed to be granted in some fashion, would give him a second chance to test his skills against the best warriors of the fairy folk.

No sooner had he thought the thought, than he heard a clash of metal, coming from a long distance away. He started to run, but then he remembered the spell Fiachna had put on his feet. If he ran again, would the enchantment return?

He could not be sure, so he kept walking—though at as brisk a pace as he could.

He was approaching a valley encircled by low hills, forming a natural amphitheater. Someone had erected poles at measured intervals around the hilltops, and various banners fluttered from these poles, each with a different color and design. Between these flags garlands of flowers were swagged, and an assortment of vendors moved around the scene, hawking their wares. They did not seem to demand any payment for their merchandise, however—whatever it was—but handed it out freely to anyone who asked.

Connla ducked under a rope of flowers and stepped forward to get a good view of the valley spread out before him.

It was a true battlefield. Pavilions made of gauzy fabric had been erected at vantage points on either side so that the ladies could watch their heroes at play. The central area was clear and level; not even a stone threatened the unwary foot. Two mighty armies met here.

One side was led by Fiachna; even at a distance, Connla could make out his hawkish face quite clearly. With him was a great company of fairy men attired in every sort of bizarre costume, waving weapons ranging all the way from swords and spears to sticks and stones.

Indeed, as Connla narrowed his eyes to peer more closely, all the weapons might have been no more than sticks and stones. But the warriors carrying them were making a great roar as if they thought themselves the best armed in the land.

The opposition had clothed itself in shimmering fabrics not unlike the coppery cloak Connla wore. Some were draped in silver, some in gold, others in robes of jewel tones. They glittered like a lady's jewel box spilled out into her lap. Their weapons also defied understanding; they might have been flowers or weeds or huge plumes from exotic birds.

If they meant to fight with such outlandish tools, where had the sound of clashing metal come from?

At that moment the two armies met and Connla had his answer. When branch struck plume, both rang like bronze. The touch of a flower stem could open a long bloody slash on an opponent's cheek. Their weapons might be fanciful, yet the damage they did appeared very real.

One of those in the jewel-robed crowd glanced up and saw Connla looking down at him.

"You there, Fiery Hair!"

Connla automatically glanced around, as if expecting someone else to be the object of that shout.

"I say, Fiery Hair! Come down and join us, we have been waging this battle for you!" The man calling up to Connla was half a head taller than those around him, and his cloak was not one color, but many. When it rippled, its hues changed with every move so that it might have been striped with green and blue and amber and brown and gold and silver and purple. As Connla started down the hill he noticed that the tall man wore a crown of gold.

"I am Finvarra, king of the Sidhe," he cried, "and this war is because of you, so you had better take part in it. Here, fight at my side." He said this last as Connla reached him, and immediately handed the young man a sword that he produced from some voluminous fold in his cloak.

At least it felt like a sword.

It looked like a reed from some quiet lake.

Connla stared down at the thing.

"Have you never used a weapon before?" Finvarra asked him with a note of scorn in his voice. "Take it up quickly and strike, foreign-born. Your Blathine is watching to see you do something brave."

Brave! Of course he would do something brave if Blathine was watching. Brandishing the sword Finvarra had just given him, he ran toward the opposing side, shouting as courageously as anyone else.

In midstride he thought: *Am I really being brave doing this, if I cannot be killed, anyway?*

But by then, the enemy was boiling around him and he was in the heart of desperate fighting.

Connla did not see Fiachna, though he would have liked to take a cut or two at the fairy man. He could run safely now, he had discovered, so the enchantment had worn off. But he still seethed with resentment for the trick Fiachna had played on him. He took this resentment out on Fiachna's comrades as best he could, acquitting himself brilliantly with a series of cuts and thrusts and slashes. The reed, or sword, or whatever it was, fitted so smoothly to his hand it seemed an extension of his own arm. Lighter in weight than any sword he had every handled, it did not make his muscles tired and seemed to operate almost with a will of its own, rising to parry an opponent's sword thrust before he even saw it, creating a dazzling net of safety around Connla's person.

"Connla, Connla!" someone was calling.

His sword was protecting him so well he dared risk a glance to the side. There he saw Blathine at the entrance to a silken pavilion, her tiny hands clasped admiringly under her chin as she watched his battle prowess.

Connla threw her a wide smile and a wink and she waved back to him, flirting a square of some delicate lavender fabric into the air. Her gesture was so graceful, so unlike any woman's he had ever seen, Connla was lost for a moment in rapt admiration of her.

In that moment Fiachna ducked under his guard and cut off his head.

Eight

ONNLA'S ONLY SENSATION was one of extreme cold as the blade of the sword severed his neck. His brain, being in his head, did not record the pumping of blood from the frenzied heart as the body emptied itself. His eyes went on seeing for a while, however, and noted the world spinning wildly around him as his head tumbled to the ground, rolled, and at last came to a stop in a tangle of grass.

Very close to the end of Connla's nose an ant paused on its journey up a blade of grass and looked at the newcomer to its territory.

Having nothing else to do, Connla looked back at it.

"Are you going to step on me?" the ant inquired. It had a suprisingly deep voice for such a tiny creature.

"I am not," Connla assured it. "I have no feet."

The ant swiveled its round little head on its thread of a neck. "So. You have no body, either."

"I have not."

"So." The ant considered this. "If I had no body, only a head, I would be dead. Are you dead?"

Connla considered this. In the Isles of the Blest, he had seen men with severed limbs recover to laugh and live. But could a decapitated man do so as well? Having lost one's head seemed horribly permanent, even in a world of magic.

"I cannot say if I am dead or not," he told the ant at last.

"Do you feel any pain? Any hunger?" asked the deep-voiced insect.

"None."

"Can you go away from this place if you like?"

"I doubt it."

"So." The ant fell silent again.

"But my mind keeps on thinking," Connla offered hopefully. "As long as I am thinking, I must be alive."

The ant pondered this. "There are many who never think, yet are considered to be alive," it said.

"Then what *is* 'being alive'?"

Coming down its grass blade, the ant ventured closer to Connla's face. It found a perch for itself on the very end of his nose, which tickled, but Connla had no fingers with which to scratch and it seemed impolite to mention his slight discomfort to his new—and perhaps last— friend. Having someone keep him company while he waited to be dead had become very important to him.

"Being alive," said the ant, "means being part of something and taking part in something. I am part of an ant colony, and I take part in the support of the colony. You—" and here the creature waved a feeler disapprovingly at what remained of Connla—"are not even part of a whole person."

"Surely there is more to being alive than that."

"Perhaps," the ant agreed. "There are others in my colony who recognize my smell, and if I did not return, they would have a small memory of me for a while. That may be a form of being alive. Are there those who would remember you?"

Connla's lips were becoming very dry, but he managed a smile. "Blathine!"

"One of the Sidhe, is it? Well, I would not count on the memory of one of the fairy folk for much," the ant warned him. "Their lives are so long and they are so wrapped up in themselves, they do not burden themselves with a lot of memories. You are—were—a mortal, were you not? Will mortals remember you?"

"My mother would." Connla started to say, then felt his eyes stinging as if he were going to cry. "But she is already dead. My father, a famous warrior called Conn of the Hundred Battles, surely remembers me."

"So you are alive," the ant said with conviction. "And you will remain so. For a while."

"For how long?"

The ant began rubbing its face with one forelimb. Obviously it had an itch of its own. "Who can say?"

&

On the Hill of Usna, Connla was indeed remembered. Conn of the Hundred Battles had aged since his son's disappearance; each season made his hair whiter and thinner, his shoulders more stooped. He had given up hope that Connla would return, for too much time had passed in the land of men. Yet there was not a day when he did not recall some favorite gesture of his son's, or catch a glimpse of some bit of polished copper that reminded him of Fiery Hair.

His chief druid was in deep disgrace. Conn blamed the druid for Connla's loss and had banished him to a bog, where the old priest had made a hut for himself from blocks of turf. Weeds sprouted on the roof, and it was usually colder and clammier inside the place than it was outside.

Hundred Battles' tribe shunned the bog, and if they were forced to go close to it, to fetch back a stray cow or pick some herb for the larder, they spat in the direction of the druid's hut and turned around three times sunwise.

Within his damp walls Coran the Druid inhaled the odor of the earth day and night, and wondered what had happened to him. From time to time he attempted some small spell in a futile effort to bring Fiery Hair back, but the spells never worked. He realized they were hopeless before he began; he only tried out of habit. And he never dared put much power behind them, for he had become afraid of his own magic—which, it seemed, was what had got him into this predicament in the first place.

If only I had not sacrificed the woman! he told himself ten tens of times, beating his skull with age-spotted fists.

As he agonized thus one day, a movement at the edge of his vision caught his attention. Glancing sideways he saw an insect, a strange bluish-green insect with an elongated body divided into three segments, and three pairs of translucent wings that glittered like quartz.

Forgetting himself, the old druid sat upright and stared at the insect. He had spent a number of seasons beside the bog, suffering the intrusion into his house of every form of pest and vermin. He had awakened to find mice nibbling at his toes in the winter and gnats trying to get into his nose and eyes in the summer. He had no love for any of the small nuisances, yet this exceedingly unusual creature interested him.

Had it been less strange, he would have taken up a clod and smashed it on the spot, before it could bite him or steal some particle of his food or make holes in his only remaining cloak.

An opalescent light began to glow around the insect. The light pulsed faintly, like a candle that flickers, strengthens, and flickers again.

Coran the Druid began to be afraid.

"What are you?" he whispered.

"Only a voice," came an answer so soft he could hardly hear it. But with the sound, the light around the insect dimmed until it almost went out, as if making sound used up all the energy the creature possessed.

"What do you want with me?"

"I need you to be brave."

Coran crouched lower in his shabby rags. "Just surviving takes all the courage I have left. I am very much in my chieftain's disfavor."

"He would restore you to your former stature if you gave him back his son."

The druid stiffened. "You have word of the boy? You know where he is?" Even as he spoke, he was saying to himself how familiar the voice sounded; surely he had heard it before. And not from an insect. But that was long ago . . . He could not say when, or who . . .

"Connla Fiery Hair still lives," the voice went on, "but you and his father must reach out to him with all the strength you possess or he will fade and be gone forever."

The druid jumped to his feet. "*How?* What spells do I use?"

"The only spell that can reach through enchantment and bridge even death," the voice answered. Then it faded. The halo of light surrounding the strange insect grew very bright for the space of a heartbeat, until it went out all at once, like a snuffed candle.

When the druid bent closer, the insect had disappeared.

"I know where I last heard that voice!" the druid exclaimed to himself. "On the hill, when the wicker was burning. The boy's own mother had that voice!"

Without waiting to put on his raggedy cloak the druid burst from his turf house and began running as fast as his tottery legs would carry him, toward the stronghold of Conn of the Hundred Battles.

From a long distance off, the sentries saw him coming. They shouted to the gatekeeper, who shouted to a servant, who shouted to Conn's steward, who eventually went to tell his master: "The former chief druid is coming."

Hundred Battles was slouched on the base of his spine on a bench covered with the skin of a huge ram. Once the wool had been white; now it was matted and stained. Only the great horns curving from the ram's head still spoke of former glory, but they were flung over the back of the bench and no one saw them.

"What can he want here?" Conn grumbled. "That man knows I would as soon kill him as look at him."

"He must have some urgent reason for daring your fort, then," the steward pointed out.

"Very well. Show him in. But warn him I am in no mood for any of his foolishness!"

The druid soon entered the hall, all bows and nods and obsequious gestures. His former aura of self-confidence was gone. Years of living on the lip of a bog had made a different man of him.

"Have you some important message for me, you old fraud?" the chieftain of Usna demanded to know.

In a halting voice, the druid related his recent experience, including his recognition of the mysterious voice. At first, Hundred Battles listened with a bored expression and tapping fingers; then he began to lean forward, and his fingers fell silent upon his knee.

"You say it was the voice of my first wife? Are you certain of this?"

"I am."

"And why would she visit you and not me?"

The druid shrugged. "You know how women are," was all the explanation he offered.

Conn of the Hundred Battles knew many things. He knew how to judge the edge of a sword and the worth of a cow; how to build a campfire so an enemy could not see it; how to pad the inside of a helmet so it did not make his head sore. But he did not know women, though he had lived among them all his life.

He had no intention of admitting this to the druid, however.

"I do know," he said with a nod. "Since she has come to you, I suppose we should make the most of it. What did she mean by a spell that can reach through an enchantment and bridge death?"

The druid had been contemplating this very question. "The only magic that answers to that description is love," he said.

"Love . . ." Conn spoke the word and left it hanging in the air in front of him. The two men stared together, as if they could see it; as if they could see its size and shape. "And just how in the name of the sun and the stars," Hundred Battles demanded to know, "are we supposed to use *love* to get my son back?"

The druid shifted from one foot to the other. "I have not had much experience with . . . love, personally," he said. "It's tricky stuff. Volatile."

"You mean you don't know how to do it. I should have expected as much."

"Ah, I can work with it," Coran hastened to assure the chieftain, noting the fires of anger mounting in Hundred Battles' cheeks. "But I warn you, I cannot guarantee the outcome."

The other snorted in disgust. "When could you ever? Still . . . I'll try, if you think there is a chance. But if you fail me again, Coran, I will have your head to decorate my walls!"

Conn of the Hundred Battles did not really have much hope of seeing his eldest son again, but he would have tried anything. Since young Connla's disappearance, the land had continued to produce well for his people—some claimed it was because of the sacrifice of Conn's wife—and he was in no danger of being deposed. But the heart was gone out of him. His other children were colorless by comparison to his memories of Connla. When he thought of them living in these buildings after he was dead, he grew depressed. He would not feel as if some part of himself were living on with them, for they were nothing like him. Only Connla had been like him.

He did not dare to hope.

But he did not dare to refuse to try, either.

"We must assemble everyone who loved your son," the druid told him. "All together in one place. The birth of the sun is the most potent time for sending messages, so we will convene on the hilltop at sunrise and you will all call out his name in a loud voice."

"You will not be calling with us?"

"I did not love him," the druid admitted honestly. "I liked him, you understand . . . but it is not the same."

"It is not the same," Conn agreed, wondering to himself how many had really loved his son and how many had only liked him. How could he be sure?

"While the call is sounded, I will build a special fire whose smoke can carry the message a long way," the druid went on. "Fiery Hair was stolen by the magic people, the fairy folk, and their lands lie very far to the west. We will have to wait until a morning when the wind is blowing in that direction—which does not often happen here."

Grimly, Conn nodded. "We will wait," he said. "We have waited this long already."

Preparations were begun. Conn ordered everyone who had known his eldest son to come to the stronghold and appear before him. He asked each person questions, endeavoring to discover the depth of their feeling for the boy.

"Ask them sharp questions," the druid had advised. "Those who really loved him will remember the small details about him; those who only pretended to love him will speak in generalities."

Coran was proven right, and to the chieftain's surprise, it appeared that those who loved his son most were not always the ones he would have expected. His other wives, his own sister, and some of his nearest kinsmen, referred to Connla as "charming," "brave," "beautiful." But his charioteer remembered a time when the boy had fallen and skinned his knee and laughed instead of crying. And the steward recalled the way Connla used to cock his head to one side when listening to the music of the harper, and the gentle smile that played around his lips at such times.

So it was that Hundred Battles learned who had really cared for his son, and when the morning finally arrived and all the portents were right, he and they gathered together on the hilltop to call out to Connla of the Fiery Hair, with love.

Nine

CONNLA'S HEAD LAY, left ear down, in the deep grass. His right ear could hear the sounds of the battle dwindling. No one came near the head; his only companion remained the ant.

But even ants have business to do. The small creature began to march purposefully down his nose, then across Connla's cheekbone. "Where are you going?" he asked it.

"To find a crumb to take to our nest," the ant replied.

"Can you not stay with me just a little longer?"

The ant said in its deep voice, "My time is not your time. If I do not go back with a crumb now, I have failed to perform my duty to my colony. If I stay here with you, someone would suffer because of me. But I wish you well," it added, just before it crawled from his face and vanished into the grass.

I left my people, Connla thought with a stab of mental pain. *Did they suffer because of me?*

He wondered if he were dead yet.

If this was death, he did not like it. He did not like having his thoughts torment him, and he did not like being alone in the grass with nothing to look at but a . . . foot.

A foot?

He rolled his eyes in his head and followed the foot upward to an ankle, wrapped in thongs made of some leafy vine. Above the ankle was the swell of a calf, and then a knee, and somewhere above that, higher than his eyes could look, was a person. Or something like a person.

"Here you are," said Finvarra.

The king of the fairy folk reached down and picked up Connla's head. He brushed the dirt off it and plucked a spear of grass from the fiery hair.

Connla tried to wet his dry lips with his still drier tongue, but it was no use. "My nose itches," he managed to say.

Finvarra grinned at him. "Scratch it," he advised. He lifted the head higher, reached out with his other hand and caught hold of something he had propped against a tree—and Connla found his head settling down onto his own two shoulders again.

There was a moment of blinding shock, like countless tiny fires racing through his body. He leaped, he twitched. Then he was whole again, gazing in astonishment at Finvarra.

"You said something about your nose, I believe?" the fairy king prompted.

Connla reached up, delighted to find he had an arm and that arm was obeying a command from his brain. At his order, his fingers performed the task he set for them, scratching his nose. What a wondrous achievement it suddenly seemed, to have an arm and a hand and fingers and to be actually able to scratch an itch! He felt like a man who had received a great gift.

The itch relieved, Connla explored his other bodily functions. He had legs and they could stand and walk. He could bend a knee, lift it, touch it with one of his wonderful hands. He could twist his torso from side to side, he could make it move forward and back, he could do countless wonderful things with a body he had always taken for granted before.

Finvarra watched him with amusement. "Everyone should be dead from time to time. It is very good for you."

"I remember seeing babies staring in delight at their own toes," Connla told him. "Now I understand how they felt." His glands were working again; saliva flooded his mouth and he was able to speak more clearly.

"Is the battle over?" he asked Finvarra.

"Indeed it is. My side won, of course. Fiachna was badly beaten for the mean trick he played on you."

"Did you kill him?"

Finvarra's face glowed. "Of course we did! I did it myself, with a great fanfare and a flourish of trumpets! There were blue swords slashing the air and blue spears singing over our heads, and songs of valor on every tongue. A great battle was fought just over that rise. We trapped a horde of Fiachna's followers there and drove them to earth like badgers. Some broke and tried to run, but most of them stood to fight, Fiachna among them.

"When all the others were slain, I, Finvarra, singled my enemy out and fought him in hand to hand combat. A great struggle it was; we tore up all the ground around us. If you had not been dead, you would have heard us."

"I was not dead," said Connla.

"Of course you were. Did I not find your head myself and restore it to your body for you? You were not permanently dead, for these are the Isles of the Blest and death is never permanent. But you were dead enough for regular purposes. Dead enough to justify Fiachna's claim of having killed you."

Stubbornly, Connla repeated, "*I was not dead.*"

The king bent a long look upon him. "You were not in the dark?"

"I was not."

"You could think?"

"I could. And hear, and speak. I had a most interesting conversation with an ant, in fact."

Finvarra shook his head. "You cannot be dead if you are going to behave in that fashion. We will not allow Fiachna to count you as his victim unless he really killed you."

"But he did cut off my head," said Connla, surprised to find himself arguing the matter from Fiachna's side.

"I'm afraid there is something wrong with you," Finvarra said disapprovingly. "You may be under some sort of protection we did not know about. I must ask Blathine; she brought you here. But you have to be governed by our laws, Fiery Hair. When you are killed you must be dead."

Connla told him honestly, "I do not mind, I suppose, since death is not permanent. But I did not try to evade it. What happened to me just happened. My head stayed alive."

The king of the fairies pursed his lips. "Bad. Very bad. There must be no magic but ours in this kingdom. Come with me. We will find Blathine and have you fixed."

The words "have you fixed" had an unpleasant ring, which Connla did not like. He tried to hang back, but Finvarra pinched his shoulder between a thumb and forefinger of astonishing strength and pulled the mortal along with him. "This is for your own good," the fairy king said.

"The last time someone claimed they were doing something for my own good," Connla protested, "they killed my mother!"

Finvarra would not listen. Irresistibly, he dragged Connla after him up a hill and across a meadow, down a slope and through a brook and up another hill, until the battlefield lay spread before them once more. The silken pavilions were still in place, the colorful banners still flying.

There were no dead bodies to be seen, of course. Everyone was up and about, talking of the war.

No time had passed.

Holding his captive firmly by the shoulder, Finvarra led him to the tent which was Blathine's. She emerged at once, so beautiful that for a moment Connla forgot his predicament, forgot everything but the exquisite creature who was smiling at him so radiantly. He reached out to her but Finvarra jerked him back.

"Not yet," said the king. "We have a problem here."

Blathine raised her eyebrows, delicate as a butterfly's antennae. "The only problem I can see is that you are keeping someone from me who wants to come to me." Her tone was icy.

"Connla was killed, well and proper," said Finvarra. "His head was cut off cleanly and rolled some distance from his body. When the battle was over I had to hunt for it, in fact, to reunite the two and give him the good news of our victory. But he had refused to die."

Blathine turned to stare at Connla, who suddenly felt guilty over this apparent breach of etiquette. "I do not *think* I was dead," he murmured. "I cannot be certain, having never been dead before. But—"

"But he could still see and hear and think, by his own admission," Finvarra interrupted. "So he was not dead. Fiachna's claim to have slain him is negated and the whole issue of the war is clouded."

"Beheading is definitely terminal," Blathine told Connla in a slow voice, looking at him hard.

"So I always thought," he assured her.

"Why did you not die?"

He searched his memory, trying to find an answer for her. "When the sword bit through my neck, I thought surely I was dead. Then—then a sort of strength seemed to come to me, from somewhere. And I found myself having a strange conversation with an ant about life and death. The ant claimed one does not die as long as one is being remembered—"

"—and loved," Blathine finished for him. "That is how it is with mortals, Finvarra! I see what has happened here. Someone in the world from which I brought Connla Fiery Hair is still thinking about him and loving him."

Finvarra was displeased. "We cannot allow it. His people should have forgotten him long ago. Just how long has he been with us, Blathine . . . in mortal time?"

The fairy woman wrinkled her brow. "I am no good at sums," she said. "But it has been many seasons. More than that; many years, I am certain. All those who knew him are old now."

Connla was shocked at her words. No time had passed! He had only been in the Isles of the Blest for this one radiant day, a day without night or weariness. How could she possibly claim that years had elapsed back home on the Hill of Usna?

"My father, Conn of the Hundred Battles," he asked eagerly. "Is he still alive?"

The expression on Blathine's lovely face changed to one of annoyance. "How would I know?"

"Can you not . . . work some magic? See him? You used to be able to see me, did you not?"

"I did. I could. But why should I? What has he to do with you now? He is an old man and you are young. You will always be young in the Isles of the Blest. Your existence goes on here with us. What happens to him does not concern you anymore."

Connla thought of the ant, hurrying to get back to its colony, where its only life was one of hard and probably thankless labor. Yet the colony *was* its life.

"I would know of my people," he said aloud.

"Perhaps you should," Finvarra agreed. "They are obviously thinking of you, so they are concerned in some way, Blathine."

She thrust out her lower lip, as ripe and red as the sweetest of cherries. "They just want to take him from me, that is why they keep interfering. We have only to wait a little longer and they will all be dead and leave us alone."

Connla said, "My mother is dead, but she has not deserted me."

"I did not desert you," Blathine reminded him. "Is she more precious to you than I am?"

"No one is more precious to me than you are," Connla said hastily. "But she is my mother. Do you not feel such ties with your own mothers?" As he asked his question, he looked from Blathine's face to that of Finvarra, but all he received in return were blank stares.

Then he remembered. Since arriving in the fairy realm he had seen no children.

"You do have mothers?"

Blathine and Finvarra looked at each other.

"We do," Finvarra said at last. "Or did. Long ago. But we live so long, we drift away from one another and form new groups, make new friendships . . . we have not been children, any of us, for a very long time."

Now they were speaking of time. Connla grasped the familiar concept eagerly. "How long? How long ago were you born? And are children ever born here any more? If so, when?" Once he began asking the questions, he could not stop. He recalled Blathine's early comment about needing no children for replacement, since no one died.

The king of the fairies stroked his jaw reflectively. "The past is a haze," he said. "The future is a mist. On the Isles of the Blest we see the Now, and that only. As for children, we occasionally have a few; a very few, just for the novelty of it, because the new ones bring such brightness with them. But birth is a most rare event among us."

"You and I could have children, then," Connla suggested to Blathine.

"A woman of the Sidhe and a mortal man? It has been done," she admitted. "But not by me. And I certainly would not consider having children with someone who defied our laws!" she added with a startling swiftness, bringing the subject back to its original point.

Finvarra nodded. "You speak wisely. You might find a child blooming in an unfolding flower, but if this Fiery Hair were its father, who can say how it would behave? We cannot welcome rebels into our land. There are enough here already," he murmured darkly.

"Connla, if you would stay here with me, you will have to become one of us in all possible ways," Blathine said. "That includes giving up your ties with the other world, the mortal world."

"I did not seek to keep them," he protested. "It just happened."

"Then we will make it un-happen," Finvarra said with determination. "We will work a great magic upon you so that no memory of the Hill of Usna or your people is left in you. We will separate you from your past as cleanly as if we made the cut with a blue sword."

Connla felt a faint shiver run up his spine. "Can you do this?" He did not like the idea of having his past cut away. He had chosen the Isles of the Blest of his own free will, he thought; that should be enough. He should not have to suffer the destruction of his memory, for there were bright places in that memory, moments of happiness and joy he did not want to lose.

He had not counted those moments among his treasures until just now, but suddenly they seemed very valuable and he clung to them with a fierce determination.

By the set of Connla's jaw, Finvarra recognized the degree of the mortal man's resistance. The king of the Sidhe sighed. "Why could you not have brought us someone easier, Blathine?"

"I did not want someone easier. Someone pliable and weak would never stand out in a crowd, but always melt into it. This one shone like a separate sun from the first moment I saw him and I wanted him and no other."

Her words filled Connla's heart with joy, for surely she was expressing a powerful love for him. But if to enjoy that love meant giving up all memory of other loves, of his parents, his homeland . . .

"You would forget all the pain you ever knew," Blathine whispered in his ear, her voice sweet enough to make stones weep. "You would never again be tormented with visions of a wicker basket burning on the Hill of Fires. No sadness would linger in your thoughts, no grief, no sense of loss. With all ties cut and your memory wiped away, you would awaken as we are—in a realm where every morn is springtime."

She ran her tiny, thrilling hands up Connla's arm to his shoulder, then bestowed the tenderest of caresses upon his face and throat. He felt a blush burn up his neck and into his cheeks. Finvarra was watching.

"Complete happiness is what we are offering you, Connla," the king of the fairy folk said. "You have only to agree to receive it. Mortals live out their brief lives and go to their graves dreaming of something that lies within your grasp, always feeling slightly cheated because they have never felt what you can feel forevermore."

"Forevermore," echoed Blathine. "And it costs so little."

"Passage must always be paid," Connla said, remembering the words Blathine had spoken to him on their journey here.

Finvarra nodded. "Indeed. But you will find this a pleasant payment. We must begin the sorceries at once, however. Just say that you agree and it will be done so smoothly, so easily, you will feel nothing." He smiled. The king of the Sidhe had a smile as bright as stars, as compelling as suns. When he smiled, his beauty was so dazzling Connla had to turn his head away.

And in the moment when he turned his head away he saw that he now stood in the center of a crowd.

The Sidhe had gathered around him in a circle many men deep. As variegated and brightly hued as a garden of flowers, they pressed in upon Connla. Each face he saw was beautiful in its own way. Some were fair, some were dark; some were plump and pink-cheeked, others were lean-featured and finely sculpted. This one had the visage of a fox, but with a merry grin. That one resembled a sea-aster growing in some salt marsh, with deep purple eyes and a mop of yellow hair atop a graceful stem of body. A third, draped in gauzy splendor, might almost have been a butterfly. But each was beautiful.

Smooth-faced, blank-eyed, beautiful.

Blank-eyed.

Connla drew in a swift breath.

In no fairy face did he catch a glimpse of memory. As effortlessly as flowers, the Sidhe lived for Now.

Finvarra stepped closer. "Just say you agree," he repeated.

Why do they need my agreement? Connla found himself wondering. Or perhaps the idea had not come from his own head at all, but from a random whisper he heard on the wind. A whisper of a familiar voice, calling to him over a great distance, asking him to question.

It might have been his mother's voice. It might have been his imagination. But he listened.

"We will not force you," Blathine said, overhearing his thoughts. "It is not our way. You must choose, Connla, for yourself. You must make this final choice."

"Why do you call this a final choice?"

Her laughter rippled like a brook skipping over stones. "Because once you are totally joined with us you will never have to make any more decisions. Does a tree make decisions? Do flowers?"

"Or reeds in a lake?" Connla interposed.

She gave him a penetrating look. "Even so. They have no choices to make because they have surrendered themselves to the natural world. So it is with us; so it will be with you. Just this one last, human decision, and you are free from all that forevermore."

Forevermore, whispered the voice on the wind.

"See what you gain in return!" cried Finvarra. With a gesture, the fairy king scattered his people. They immediately fell to enjoying themselves in the countless ways of the Sidhe, all within Connla's sight. Some formed musical groups, playing harps and lyres and pipes in irresistible harmony. One band of men brought forth trumpets of some shiny metal more white than silver, more bright than gold, and blew resonant notes that tugged at the very roots of Connla's soul.

Captured by the music, others began to dance. Fairy women in gowns as light as gossamer whirled and spun, holding out their delicate hands to entice various partners. Their hair drifted on the soft air as if it lay on water. Their round limbs were unfailingly graceful, and the joy they brought to the dance almost swept Connla's heart away.

Beyond musicians and dancers, another party was spreading what appeared to be a east. "But I thought there was no need for eating here . . ." Connla said.

"Eating can be enjoyed as pure pleasure, and in that way we sometimes celebrate the delights of food," Blathine told him. "See what has been prepared! Pitchers of honey-wine await us, and platters heaped with fruits unlike any you have seen before. When we wish to dine, we take our choice from the rarest products of the earth, since distance is no problem for us. And we have bakers who know how to turn grain into cakes so delicious and sweet they begin to melt as soon as your fingers touch them. The most delicate of foods await our pleasure, Connla. Do you not hunger for them?"

To his surprise, he did. The appetite he had not felt since he ate the hare on the island rose up in him as if bidden by Blathine's words, and his mouth watered. He saw the fairy folk spreading soft coverlets upon the grass and sitting down, passing the food from one to another, eating, laughing, kissing crumbs from the lips of their neighbors.

"I am hungry," he admitted.

"We will eat, then," Blathine assured him. "As soon as you agree."

"Agree?" He frowned; he had almost forgotten.

"To the sorcery for severing you from your past," Blathine said. "It must be done soon, Fiery Hair, or there is much you will be denied." She gave him a long-lidded, lazy look, and he remembered the bower where he had held her in his arms. He remembered every detail of it, every sensation, every giving and taking.

"I want to!" he said. "Ah, Blathine, I want to so much. But it is as if . . . as if invisible hands are holding me back . . ." He tried to put all his longing in his eyes so she could see it.

She stood so close to him her soft breath was in his nostrils. Setting one gentle hand on either side of his face, she searched his eyes with her own. Then she turned toward Finvarra.

Her voice was sad as she said, "My Connla Fiery Hair is not quite ready."

"Mortals are stupid and stubborn," Finvarra said. "I cannot understand them. They seem determined to hurt themselves."

Blathine nodded. "It is so. But we will not give up on this one, for he is too dear to me."

She turned back to Connla. "We will dance with the dancers," she told him, "and sing with the singers. And when you are ready to eat the feast which has been prepared for you in my kingdom, you will tell me."

He understood her meaning. His first bite of food would be his agreement. No sooner had he realized this than his treacherous stomach began growling, demanding to be fed.

Connla gritted his teeth.

Blathine did not press the point, but took his hand and led him toward the nearest group of dancers.

The music caught his feet like a net. Without any thought on his part, his feet took up the steps of the dance as if they had always known them; as if the fairies' dance were an ancient pattern he had been born knowing.

છ૭

"I almost caught a glimpse of him just then!" Coran the Druid cried.

"Where, where?" Conn of the Hundred Battles shouldered forward, taking up the druid's space, trying to see with his eyes.

At the old chieftain's command, all those who had loved his son had assembled at the Hill of Usna. The druid had formed them into a circle, like the ancient circles of standing stones that dotted the land and still vibrated with long-ago powers. Holding hands and chanting. Connla's friends had tried to summon a vision of him. And because it was not natural for them to stand perfectly still for a long period of time, they had begun to move their feet in a rhythm, a step; a dance.

"There, there he is!" the druid shouted exultantly, waving the ash stick he always carried.

A mist seemed to rise on the Hill of Usna, filling the center of the ring of people. In that mist there were other dancers, seen dimly at first; then growing clearer. But these dancers were moving with wild abandon, weaving in and out as if they were making a tapestry of the color and grace of their bodies.

Among them, clearly visible for one heartbeat, was an exceptionally tall figure with hair the color of flame.

"Connla, my son!" old Hundred Battles yelled with all his might.

 confound

In the heat of the dance, Connla paused. At once, Blathine tugged at his arm, urging him to move closer to her and make his steps more lively. Still he hesitated. "I thought I heard someone call me," he said.

"You heard nothing. Wind in the trees, perhaps."

"Not wind. A voice, a voice I know . . ."

"You see? Memories are haunting you again and making you sad. Be wise, my Connla, and make yourself happy by renouncing your past forever! Come with me now to the feast and let me feed you some of our fine soft bread made with currants. I will hold it to your lips with my own fingers, just so." She bunched her dainty little fingertips together and, laughing, held them up to his mouth, trying to distract him. The musicians played louder and the dancers spun more gaily, trying to make

Connla forget the voice he had heard. But he would not forget.

෴

"He is fading, he is gone," Hundred Battles mourned. "Bring him back, Coran!"

Flushed with success, the druid was delighted to have achieved so much. Being able to actually see young Fiery Hair in the fairy realm, if only for a moment, was more than he had expected. But at the chieftain's urging he doubled his efforts, chanting exhortations, drawing patterns in the air with his ash stick, directing the people to bend their bodies this way and that in a reconstruction of the dance.

Once more, the mist formed in the center of the circle on the Hill of Usna. Darker this time, more opaque, it revealed little, only a hint of moving forms within.

Conn of the Hundred Battles made a move as if to hurl his body into the mist, but his druid caught him by the tunic and held him back. "You must not do that, you would be destroyed."

"Let me go, you old wart-faced fool! My son is there."

"Your son is so far away there is no way to measure the distance. It is only his image you see, and if you try to join with it, you will be lost somewhere between here and the Isles of the Blest. Even I would not have enough power to summon you back, and I have no doubt the Sidhe would not make you welcome in their realm either."

Conn continued to struggle, though with diminished effort. The mist was fading again. Dimly, he perceived his own people beyond it, on the other side of the circle.

The old man slumped to his knees, covering his face with his hands. "I just wanted one more look at my son's face," he said.

The druid bent over him, moved by pity. "You shall see him again," Coran promised. "There is a gateway, we know that much now. We will keep striving to reach your son and someday we may bring him back for you."

A haggard face looked back at him. Hundred Battles bore little resemblance to the dauntless warrior of earlier fame. He was a man of great age and getting older, with all his victories and all his defeats scored across his features like the roads of a well-used land. "Bring him back," he pleaded. "Bring my son back to me while there is enough life left in me to see him. I have so little time."

Ten

BLATHINE WAS WISE. She eventually abandoned her efforts to make Connla of the Fiery Hair agree to the sorceries that would make him forget his people. She guessed, to the width of a clipped lizard's hair, just how far he could be pushed, and she did not push that tiny bit farther which would have turned him against her. Instead, when he continued to resist, she smiled and bided her time, for Blathine was free of the relentless pressure of the seasons as they sped by.

On the Isles of the Blest, no time passed.

No one grew sick, no one died—except for brief moments of velvety blackness that faded quickly, leaving only a sense of refreshing sleep behind. Between the splendid battles of the heroes, these brief respites took place.

Only Connla did not share them, for no matter how badly he was wounded, he could not die even briefly.

But he learned to enjoy the fighting. Since he did no one permanent harm, he could use his skills to the utmost, and he proved himself a master of strategy. His sometime enemy Fiachna was so impressed he introduced the human man to the techniques of the Blue Sword. These consisted of complete sets of stylized maneuvers involving jewel-hilted weapons with rippled blades, and mastering them required a grace Connla had never learned on the battlefields of Erin.

When not engaged in war one could always seek amusement with friends. Connla's best friend was the pointy-eared little chap known as Whimsical, who took it upon himself to be at the human's elbow whenever Connla desired masculine companionship.

Whim was a storyteller by nature. He boasted of knowing every joke that had ever been made by one of the Sidhe, and a great number of jokes from the world of mortals as well. To entertain Connla, he ran through a whole repertoire of tales that made the fairy folk laugh, but Connla could find nothing even faintly amusing in any of them.

Whim confessed to being baffled by this. "Perhaps your people and mine do not have the same sense of humor," he said finally.

"I think not," Connla agreed. "Tell some of the funny stories you have learned from listening to humans and I believe you will see the difference."

Whim obliged with jokes he swore were of human origin, but they were no funnier to Connla, though the little fairy man could hardly complete some of them for laughing.

His laughter dwindled away, however, when he realized Connla was not chuckling along with him. "No good?"

Connla shook his head. "No good. Not a giggle. Not a smile. Are you certain those were supposed to be jokes?"

Whim looked downcast. "Perhaps I've misremembered some of them. I am certain they were funny when I first heard them. But you know how it is, things slip away from you." The poor little fellow was so crestfallen, Connla felt very sorry for him.

"Everyone's memory fails them from time to time," he said. Then he thought: a memory is a hard thing to hold onto, even when one tries. So it must have value. Should I be willing to surrender mine?

He felt a gentle touch and looked down. Whim had patted his hand, ever so lightly. The fairy man's oversized eyes were brimming with sympathy. "I was not always one of these," he said in a low voice, waving his hand to indicate the carefree group capering nearby. "I began as a human too, you know."

"You did?" Connla asked in astonishment. To his eyes, Whim had seemed a perfect model for one of the Sidhe, fanciful and sprightly and otherworldly.

"I did. There was a time when I knew hunger and thirst and how to cry. You have to know how to cry before you can appreciate laughter. But I thought the life I knew was too hard. It was a long-ago life, I think. Many—what do you call them? years?—many years before your grandfather's grandfather was born. I wept and gnashed my teeth over the shortness of life as I knew it, and its brutality. One of the fairy folk overheard me and came to tell me of the Isles of the Blest.

"Never had I dreamed such a place might exist. I told my family and my friends, and at first they doubted me. But finally they came to believe. They never believed as strongly as I did, however, or yearned so hard.

"Then the Magic One came back and offered to bring me here. Something terrible . . . I do not remember what, of course . . . had just happened in my life, and so I agreed without hesitation. Almost before I knew it, I was here.

"At first it was hard for me, as it is for you. Ah, you smile, but I can tell. I've stood where you stand. Only when I agreed to give up being human altogether, could

I put all my sadness behind me." He grinned a sudden, gaptoothed grin, demonstrating his cheerfulness.

"In order to shed your sadness . . . did you have to give up some memories?"

"I did, of course. That's why I understand the struggle going on within yourself. But surely you are burdened with sad memories, just as I was. Letting go of them was like putting down a huge burden and I have never regretted it. I do seem to have lost memory with memories, however," Whim added. "Perhaps that is why I cannot tell jokes in a way to make you laugh; I do not quite remember the trick of language or point of view to make them funny for you. But here comes Blathine! Listen while I tell her one of my tales; I'll wager I can make *her* laugh."

So Whim told a joke to Blathine, a long and complicated story that made no point Connla could see. Yet she laughed. She threw back her head and laughed as if she had never heard so funny a tale.

Whim threw Connla a triumphant glance. "I do not remember how to make humans laugh, but I can always amuse the Sidhe."

The fairy folk do, indeed, have a different sense of humor, Connla thought. Then he remembered Whim's remark: "You have to know how to cry before you can appreciate laughter." In giving up his painful memories, little Whim had given up his ability to cry. Without tears to balance the scale, laughter had no meaning—at least not for a human audience.

After that, Connla was careful to at least smile whenever Whim told one of his jokes, and sometimes Fiery Hair managed a laugh he did not feel. But not for all the rainbows would he have hurt his little friend's feelings.

And soon—because he did indeed have a very limited memory—Whim forgot that Connla had ever failed to be amused by his stories.

Everything painful can be forgotten, the young man reminded himself. And how easily! All I have to do is agree, as Finvarra and Blathine have urged me to do . . .

Yet still he hesitated, though he could not say why.

Then the dragon came.

Connla was with Blathine in her bower when the sky began to darken. He had grown so used to its unfailing light that he glanced up in surprise. The fairy woman also looked up, and bit her lip.

She pulled slightly away from Connla and got to her feet.

"What is it, Blathine? Is night coming at last?"

"There is no night here," she replied impatiently, but it was obvious her thoughts were on something else; something which made a tiny little vertical line appear between her feathery eyebrows.

The tone of her voice carried a hidden warning. Connla also rose, and picked up the blue sword Fiachna had given him. He always laid his sword down upon entering Blathine's bower, for it seemed out of place there. But when its hilt was nestled into his hand he felt better, tilting his head back and watching the shadows creep across the sky. "If not night, what it it?"

"Something darker than the darkest night," she answered absently. "If any of our people are out on the sea, or in the spaces between worlds—" Breaking off abruptly, she left the bower and began running, lightfooted as a fawn, in the direction of the distant spires marking Finvarra's palace.

Connla followed her, sword at the ready.

He had never entered the palace of the king of the Sidhe, though he and Blathine had passed it many times. He understood it was forbidden to him until he was fully a member of the fairy tribe. Like the banquet food, the royal palace was only for initiates.

Or so he had thought. But when they got there this time, Blathine seized his hand and pulled him after her, right between the two guards who stood at the gateway. Neither protested; they, too, were standing with their heads tilted back, looking up at the changing sky.

Blathine strode purposefully forward, leading Connla up a flight of broad stone steps bordered with a bewildering array of flowers blooming in alabaster pots. At the top of the steps a great gilded door swung silently open at their approach.

Connla stepped into Finvarra's palace and a great sense of wonder overtook him.

So far, all his experiences on the Isles of the Blest had been in the open air, beneath the azure sky. Without rain or cold or cloud, the fairy folk needed no roofs. But a king must have a palace, even when the climate does not require it, and the king of the Sidhe had a palace like no other.

It seemed to be built of coral, its walls glowing with every shade of pink and creamy yellow and palest apricot. There were no windows; a series of archways served as both interior doors and openings onto little enclosed courtyards a-riot with flowers. The floor was carpeted with more blossoms, and still others had been woven into gorgeous tapestries hung everywhere on the walls. Some were purple, shading from the darkest hue to a pale and delicate lavender. Others were predominantly red—rose-pink and wine-red and a vivid scarlet. Yellows and blues and greens, and the fresh crisp touch of white, mingled with these blankets of living color so that each chamber of the palace offered fresh delights for the eye.

Each chamber also had its own musician. These were generally harpers, who sat in a corner facing outward, with magnificent harps of gold and precious woods cradled on their knees. Their music seemed a part of the perfume of the flowers and the sweetness of the gently stirring air. An occasional piper offered a note of variety, sending one clear, bright rill of music after another through the maze of rooms.

Indeed, the chambers of the palace hardly seemed to be rooms at all, but merely enclosed versions of Blathine's bower, places that were neither inside nor outside. Walking through them was like walking through a succession of brilliant soap bubbles surrounded by sheer and ephemeral color that might dissolve if one attempted to touch it.

"I have never seen a place like this," Connla breathed in awe.

"There is no place like this," Blathine told him, though her thoughts were still very much elsewhere.

They went on, through still more chambers; down long passageways where it was as bright as the day outside, though there were no wall-torches; through more chambers again; across courtyards, up stairs and down; through archways and turnings. The palace was vast, more so than Connla had ever imagined. Seen from outside, in passing, it was just an assemblage of delicate spires and slender towers. Within, it was more like a city—though Connla had never seen a city.

There was a constant flow of fairy servitors moving through Finvarra's spacious palace. Someone was always brushing past Blathine and Connla as they advanced. Servants trotted about importantly, carrying silver trays laden with flacons and goblets of crystal, or golden bowls heaped with fruit, or shining caskets that might contain jewels or magic. Everyone was a-bustle.

"They have not looked outside," Blathine muttered. "They do not know—yet."

"Know what? What is coming?"

"Wait until we find Finvarra," was all Blathine would tell him.

At last they entered a passageway much wider than the others, with a tall pair of doors at the far end. These, too, opened as if by invisible hands, and a great audience chamber yawned before Connla and Blathine.

Here was the throne of the king of the Sidhe, and an equally fine high seat for his queen. Each glittered with jewels; each was cushioned with silk.

Both were empty.

Blathine looked around in distress. "Finvarra!" she cried. "Where are you?"

"Here, of course."

Connla and the fairy woman spun around to find the king standing behind them, having entered the hall on their heels.

"What do you seek with me?" Finvarra demanded to know.

"Have you seen the sky?"

His eyes were somber. "I have."

"What are we to do?" Blathine asked nervously. Connla had never seen her show any sign of anxiety before.

"I am already attending to the matter," Finvarra assured her. "I have sent messengers to those of our people who are scattered in far places, urging them to hurry to the Isles of the Blest until the Time of the Dragon has passed."

Connla stepped forward. "What dragon? What are you talking about?"

The king glanced at the sword in the young man's hand. "I am glad you are a skilled warrior," he said. "Perhaps Blathine did not act so unwisely after all, bringing you here."

"I am glad to hear you admit it," the fairy woman interjected tartly.

Finvarra gave her a silencing look. To Connla he said, "You have not yet agreed to let us cut the bonds that tie you to your human kin, have you?"

"I have not," the other answered uneasily. He was not certain what this had to do with the dragon; he was not even certain what a dragon was, for there were no dragons in his homeland.

"So you still have your memories," Finvarra mused. "That is good, good. Do you remember fear, my fiery-haired friend? Do you remember being afraid to die? To really die, to go into a blackness you did not understand and from which you did not know how to return?"

Connla shuddered. He came of a warrior race that did not like to admit fear. But the eyes of the king were compelling. "I do remember," he said in a low voice.

"Good," Finvarra repeated. "On the Isles of the Blest we have no fear, for our warriors know they cannot actually be slain. Without fear, there is no real courage. It is a small price to pay, but a price.

"Now we have need of someone who still possesses real courage. Someone who, if he leaves the Isles of the Blest, can be killed and knows it."

"But I thought—"

"You thought wrong," Blathine interrupted. "You are not yet one of the ever-living, Connla. Only here. When you pass beyond the circle of enchantment that surrounds our homeland, you are as mortal as any other human born. You have not yet fully joined us, remember?"

He began to guess the shape of the thing they wanted him to do.

Finvarra crossed the hall and sat heavily upon his jeweled throne. His face had always looked ageless, but now his eyes seemed incredibly old. Blathine and Connla stood before him as he explained, "There are limits to all powers, even those of the Sidhe. We have a safe place here, and when we travel to other realms we can protect ourselves there too, to some extent. But there are forces quite beyond our strength; forces our greatest magic cannot turn aside.

"Such a force is the dragon.

"Every kingdom and every people, whether mortal or fairy, has known the dragon. It has many different names and many different faces, but its purpose is always the same. Destruction for the sake of destruction.

"The gods create; the dragon destroys." Finvarra slumped lower on his throne.

Blathine made a tiny sound of distress and put the back of her hand against her mouth.

Connla felt his grip tighten automatically on the hilt of his sword.

"Some are attacked by the dragon in the guise of a wild animal," Finvarra went on. "Mortals are terrified of wild animals, of the savagery they perceive lurking just beyond the light of their fires. In other instances, the dragon comes to them as famine—you almost saw the dragon on the Hill of Usna, Connla of the Fiery Hair."

"And I helped my father turn it back," Connla said, suddenly understanding.

"The Sidhe does not fear wild animals or famine," the king said. "But the great storm that arises from the sea, that is our dragon. It only happens rarely, so rarely that many generations of human men may be born and live out their spans and perish without ever noting such an event.

"But when the dragon stirs in its lair beneath the sea and lashes its mighty tail, islands rise and sink, cities die beneath the waves, mountains burst through the earth, seas boil away . . . all is changed.

"Even the Isles of the Blest are vulnerable to the dragon. This may be a small disruption, it may endanger only those beyond our immediate protection. Or it could be worse. It could be something that has only happened once before, even within the life spans of the fairy folk. It could be the death and birth of continents, and if that should happen, all our enchantments might not be sufficient to keep the waves of the cold ocean from washing over our kingdom."

"What is to be done?" Connla wanted to know.

"We will create a special sorcery just for you, to enable you to go to the ocean floor and the lair of the dragon. You will confront it with all your human bravery as well as the magical battle skills you have learned here, from us. You will not be able to slay the dragon, for it is truly immortal. But if you are very clever and very quick, you may cripple it for a while, and hold back disaster for many generations.

"Disaster not only for us, but for the lands of mortal men," Finvarra added.

"But you have many able warriors."

"None who will fight as hard as you will, Connla. None who could be as frightened as you will be."

"Do I have any choice?" the young man asked.

Finvarra nodded. "You are not yet one of us, so you do still have a choice. You can refuse. If you do, we who have no choice must wait for whatever comes, even if it is the destruction of the Isles of the Blest."

Connla turned to Blathine. Her face was pale and composed. "If I do this thing, can I really be killed?" he asked her.

"You can."

"Would you weep for me, Blathine?"

She stared at him. He—almost—thought he glimpsed an unfamiliar sparkle of moisture in the corner of her eye. Then she shook her head. "I do not weep," she told him.

"Do you love?"

Again she stared at him. But before she could answer, the chamber darkened significantly, as if all light had been bled from the outside world.

"The dragon is stirring!" Finvarra said. "Hurry, Connla, you must decide before it is too late to act."

He looked at Blathine again, trying to puzzle it all out and understand. This was not like the tests he had undergone during their journey to the Isles of the Blest; he could see now how simple those tests had been, though he still did not know what they had proven. But the threat of the dragon was terrifying and all-embracing; even Blathine was menaced by it. And his own people too, perhaps. The people he still remembered, the people he had been unwilling to forget.

"Tell me what you want me to do, Finvarra."

A look of relief spread over the face of the king of the Sidhe. He clapped his hands together three times and a flock of servants, twittering like birds, ran into the hall. They carried armor of a strange blue-white metal, which they buckled onto Connla's body and covered again with his coppery cloak. On his head they placed a plumed helmet that fitted his skull as neatly as if it had been poured over it. His feet they shod with boots so heavy he could hardly bend his knees, and through his belt they thrust an assortment of knives and darts and leather slings.

When the young warrior was fully equipped, Finvarra got up and circled him slowly, examining him from every angle. Then the king raised his hands over Connla's head and closed his own eyes. In a voice like thunder he chanted a ritual in an unknown tongue, a ritual so powerful, Connla could feel the weight of it descend upon his flaming hair and press him to the ground.

No time passed, yet the king's voice went on and on, weaving spells of sorcery.

At last there was silence.

Connla lay at full length on the floor, cushioned by the carpet of flowers. For the first time since coming to the Isles of the Blest he felt weary in every bone and sinew. When Finvarra extended a hand to help him rise to his feet, it cost the young man a great effort to do so. But once he was standing he began to feel better.

"I thought I was being crushed," he said.

"I heaped so much magic upon you it would have crushed a lesser man," Finvarra told him. "It only remains to be seen whether this is enough to protect you. We will not know until you face the dragon."

"When will that be?"

The room was so dark Connla could hardly see the king's face as Finvarra replied, "Now."

Eleven

HE FLOOR OF the fairy palace seemed to dissolve beneath Connla's feet. He felt himself sinking down *through* it, dragged lower and lower by the weight of his boots. Looking up, he could see Finvarra and Blathine above him as his eyes sank below the level of their feet. Then his vision of them was obscured by the carpet of flowers and by the coral floor itself, closing up behind him as he passed through it.

Still he sank down.

He moved through a dark, moist warmth, like a tunnel in the earth. His speed never varied, though he could not judge exactly how fast it was. But he spent what must have been a score of heartbeats or more in the darkness, before that too was left behind and he found himself in an environment of limpid aquamarine light.

Fish drifted past him, goggling at him curiously. Giant ferns waved at him as he passed by. He was in water; under water, falling down through water. Yet he had no sensation of drowning; he was able to breathe normally, as if encased in an envelope of air.

Finvarra's magic, Connla thought gratefully.

The water became darker. He sensed that it was growing very cold, though the air surrounding him remained warm enough to keep him comfortable. The fishes he saw were of unfamiliar shapes now, and startlingly large sizes. Some were very flat, as if the pressure of the water had rolled them out like dough.

Monstrous formations of stone became faintly visible through the gloom. They rose like giant canyons around him as he still went down and down and down.

The darkness became stifling. He could see nothing; he only occasionally felt something brush past him, some deep-sea creature whose size and shape he could only guess. Each touch left him shuddering with horror.

Down and down and down.

Then the dark faded again, though not as the result of any light from the sea's surface. Looking down, Connla could make out a long, sinuous form directly below him, stretched out on the pale and sandy sea bottom. The light seemed to come from this shape, pulsing with sullen and sinister hues of dull red and sulfurous yellow.

The thing was huge, running along the bottom of the sea like a giant fissure in the very fabric of the world. Just seeing it was enough to make Connla's soul go cold, in spite of the fairy warmth encircling him.

He became aware of the immensity of the sea, and his own tininess. What was he doing, a mortal, on such a mission? He had only his wits and his skills and his fear to match against some preternatural monster whose nature he could not ever hope to understand. Separated from the surface and the green land by so much distance, the fate of those above seemed less important to him. The Isles of the Blest, the Hill of Usna—they were far away. Only the dragon was here. Waiting for him.

The dragon raised its head and looked up, watching him descend.

Connla tried to get a good look at it. If he must fight the creature, he at least wanted to know what he was fighting. But his first glimpse of its eyes so shocked him that he made no attempt to examine the rest of its face. If it had a face.

The eyes were two green pools of undiluted malevolence.

Destruction was the dragon's only purpose, Finvarra had said. Seeing those eyes, Connla believed him.

As he drew nearer to it, the dragon opened its great maw and roared.

The thin casing of air around Connla stank of sulfur, making him sneeze, turning his stomach.

With a lithe twist of its monstrous body, the dragon rolled to one side to wait for Connla, opening its mouth still wider to receive him. He saw that he was falling straight into that gaping cavern, lit from within by lurid fires. Huge black teeth like polished obsidian yawned on either side of the opening, waiting to crush his body as he passed through. A curious tongue, long and thin and forked, darted in and out of the dragon's mouth as if already tasting Connla. The creature pulsed more brightly, celebrating its appetite.

Connla drew his knees up against his chest and twisted his body, then kicked out as hard as he could, propelling himself through the water at an angle so that he dropped onto the sand beside the dragon instead of into its waiting mouth.

The creature was slow, as all huge things are slow. Connla was already on his feet, with his sword balanced in his hand, before it realized its prey had not fallen into its mouth. The dragon rolled over again, roiling the water and stirring up a great mass of sand which temporarily blinded Connla. Arching its long neck, the monster looked around for the morsel of food it was anticipating.

In its hunger, it had left its mouth open and ready. Though the sight of that red light emanating from the beast's interior frightened him more than anything else, Connla made himself approach the gaping jaws. If he did not attack successfully, the dragon would surely attack him and he would die. Of such knowledge was his courage born.

Taking a step forward with bent knee, he flung a succession of darts into the dragon's mouth. Each one stabbed and stung the lining of that mouth, and tiny spurts of greenish blood stained the water.

The dragon shook its head with annoyance and closed its jaws. Once more it lifted its huge, muscular neck, and swung the heavy head around. This time it saw Connla on the sand, feet apart and braced, sword uplifted.

With a moan of delight, the dragon reached forward to swallow him.

But Connla was too quick. Using his small size to good advantage he flung himself beneath the outthrust head and wriggled into the sand. The dragon's jaws snapped shut harmlessly above him.

The creature raised its head, rolling its tongue around in its mouth and trying to taste the man. But he was not there to be tasted.

This time the dragon's roar was mixed with anger.

Half-buried in sand, Connla squirmed until he was lying on his back with the sword braced against his chest. Then he forced its point upward, until it was angled between his body and that of the dragon.

He knew his strength was not enough to drive the blade into the creature's vast body. Its skin was some unfamiliar combination of leather and scales and stony flakes of overlapping material that looked impenetrable.

But as Connla knew, the most stoutly armored being has a weak spot somewhere, and he hoped that in the case of the dragon that weak spot was its belly. So he held the sword pointing up at the monster and waited until it shifted its own massive weight downward. When it did, it would impale itself on the rippled blue blade.

If it did not—if it merely stayed as it was, crouched and waiting for him—he was trapped underneath it, in water and sand and terror.

The dragon was quiet.

Connla guessed it must be looking for him, rolling its fearsome eyes but wasting no energy in thrashing around until it spotted its prey. How long would it lie so? He had no way of knowing; he knew nothing about dragons or their habits. Perhaps, like the tiny lizards who were his homeland's only reptiles, it could stay immobile for a day, if it was warm and comfortable.

Was it warm? Was it comfortable? Was it even a reptile?

Suddenly Connla realized just how very much he wanted to live. There were so many things still to learn, so many things he was curious about, so many things he had yet to experience! Fear of being destroyed with his life unlived swept over him. Despair was worse than the terror of the dragon.

Despair could destroy him even if the dragon did not.

He gritted his teeth. He tightened his shoulder muscles. He remembered the reeds, who had taught him that all living things have the ability to communicate.

Like a barbed dart he flung a thought at the mighty hulk above him. Rest, he thought. Rest. Sink deeper and wait.

Sink deeper.

Deeper.

Fear and grief for himself closed his throat, but his mind went on sending its message in one last, desperate effort.

Above Connla, the dragon stirred.

Shifting its vast bulk, it prepared to settle more deeply into the sea bottom and rest. Its dim brain perceived the need to rest, for soon it planned to surge upward to the surface, to leap into the sky, to make one of its rare and spectacular appearances on the surface of the world, bringing with it storm and tidal wave and destruction.

But first, a little rest. A gathering of strength.

The dragon settled down.

Its weight came to rest on the point of Connla's sword, paused, then sank deeper. Whatever its tough surface was composed of resisted the magical blue metal for a moment, then yielded, and the sword sank into the dragon's body.

A great gush of foul-smelling greenish fluid poured from the pierced body cavity. Hot as fire, it swept like a tide around Connla, washing him, and the sand beneath the monster, to one side. He could see nothing but the thick ichor of the creature and a swirl of sand, yet he sensed he was no longer under the dragon and took a great, relieved gulp of air from the protective layer around him. His throat opened again with the possibility of life.

The dragon writhed. The water around it boiled. A sense of pain, of invasion, reached the dragon's awareness, summoning fury. Once again it roared and the whole sea bed shook with the force of its voice. Vibrations moving through the water propelled Connla upward. He began kicking his legs as hard as he could, swimming toward the surface.

Below him the dragon convulsed in pain.

The ocean heaved.

The dragon could not be slain, Finvarra had said, but it could be wounded. Though Connla's sword was tiny by comparison to the dragon's immeasurable size, it had pierced a vulnerable portion of the monster and allowed the blue ice of Sidhe magic to pour into the fiery furnace of the creature's heart. The result was an interior chaos from which the dragon would be a long time recovering.

In its throes, however, it did much damage. Struggling not to be swept completely away by the turbulence around him, Connla wondered if the convulsions within the sea were being reflected on land.

Land!

The Isles of the Blest!

The Hill of Usna!

The young man clawed his way upward through the wild water. He had left the sword buried in the dragon, to continue doing whatever damage it could, so his hands were free. Instinct taught him to use them like paddles, pushing the water away from him. His muscular legs churned it into a froth as he kicked, and he knew he was making progress, for he gradually perceived a dim light overhead; the light of the upper world.

He was no longer alone. All around him appeared the denizens of the deep, fish and sea mammals and strange creatures somewhere between plant and animal, all struggling to escape the mighty roaring and the rending of the ocean. In their fear, even the predators of the sea did not attack their natural prey, but all rushed for the surface together, Connla in their midst.

Up and up and up.

Light now, and a change in the temperature of the water. He could sense it growing warmer and saw myriad bubbles dancing in it. One more tremendous kick and he shot upward. Then his head broke the surface and he found himself in a trough of waves.

One huge wave, grey-green and glossy, bent toward him, ready to thunder down upon him. The struggles of the dragon under the sea were already being reflected on the ocean's surface. Only when he had taken his first lungful of open air did Connla realize how exhausted he was, and wonder where land might lie . . . and if he could hope to reach it.

ᏋᎧ

On the Hill of Usna, the druid circle had been formed again. Coran the chief druid, now partially restored to Hundred Battles' favor, summoned the group at every sunrise to call out to Fiery Hair and try to reach him again. They danced in a pattern that had begun to seem very natural, almost inevitable, and as they danced they chanted.

The pattern they formed was like the scallop of a shell or the wave of the sea, and the chant they repeated was as deep and rolling as the ocean's roar.

ᏋᎧ

Swimming desperately, Connla felt something clamp on his tiring body. At first he thought it must surely be the dragon, risen to the surface to take its revenge. But no teeth pierced him; no jaws closed over him. Instead he felt as if a big fist closed ever so gently on him and carried him forward, and mixed with the wind and the waves and the roaring in his ears was a sound like human voices. There was a note in them so familiar that tears sprang to his eyes.

"I am coming," he managed to call out, though as soon as he opened his mouth a wash of sea water burned his tongue with salt. "I am coming!"

He was hurled through the water, and then he found himself—all at once—cushioned by foam. The roar behind him faded, the hiss of a gentle surf filled his ears. His feet grated on stone and sharp shells and he stood up, knee-deep in the incoming tide.

Staggering, grinning, unable to believe he was still alive and had reached land, Connla found himself on a glittering white beach and saw the host of the Sidhe awaiting him.

Finvarra was in the lead. The stern expression had vanished from the face of the fairy king. His smile was like the sun breaking through clouds; the hands he extended to welcome Connla met behind the young man's back to form a bone-crushing hug.

"You have wounded the dragon!" Finvarra cried, laughter bubbling through his voice. "The storm that it meant to savage the world with has abated. Look! The sky is light again!"

Turning his head in the king's embrace, Connla saw that the sky was as blue and tranquil as it had always been above the Isles of the Blest. The sea still heaved, however; evidence of the struggle going on in its depths.

"There will be high waves everywhere and some damage done to shores not protected by magic," Finvarra said. "But the Isles of the Blest will not be swallowed by the sea, not this time, Fiery Hair. We are in your debt. Come, a great celebration is already being arranged in your honor."

Looking past Finvarra, Connla saw Blathine smiling. Never had she been so radiant. Her skin was as luminous as a lily petal with the moon gleaming behind it. Her eyes were filled with promises that made Connla dizzy.

Or perhaps he was only still tired.

Yet, could a man feel exhaustion on the Isles of the Blest?

"We can fix that for you at once," Finvarra said, hearing his silent question. The king lifted his hand from Connla's shoulder and laid it on the young man's head, and at once his tiredness fell from him like a discarded cloak.

Finvarra nodded in satisfaction. "Come now, our hero, and be welcomed as is your due."

He led Connla toward a rolling green hillside above the beach, where the familiar silken pavilions had already been set up. The sound of music came drifting toward them, overriding and canceling the voice of the troubled sea. Flower perfumes wafted on warm air, replacing the stink of sulfur in Connla's nostrils. Laughter and song filled his ears, silencing the memory of the dragon's roar.

A small hand slipped in his announced Blathine at his side.

"You were wonderful," she said worshipfully.

"I was afraid," he had to admit.

"Ah, indeed, but that made you fight all the harder, did it not?"

He nodded. He had fought hard; harder, apparently, than any of the Sidhe would have done, else one of their number might have been sent on this most dangerous of undertakings. So there was something in his human-ness more powerful even than the magic of the fairy folk . . .

Before his thoughts could pursue this path too far, Blathine leaned her warm body against his, whispering silvery things in his ear, stirring his fiery hair with her sweet breath. And the Sidhe surrounded him, burying him in their beauty.

Little Whim came up with a shy smile. "May I touch you?"

Connla laughed. "A fairy man wants to touch a mortal?"

"For luck," said Whimsical.

Shaking his head with amusement, Connla understood. Each of the Sidhe then came forward in turn to touch him with an extended forefinger. Their eyes, already larger than mortal eyes, were wider than ever as they made contact with whatever magic it was they thought lay within Connla.

He felt the tingling he had felt before when touched by one of the fairy folk. But this time the tingling seemed to be going out from him instead of coming in to him.

They did not allow him time to think of this, either. He was soon swallowed up by festival, garlanded with flowers, the center of so much attention and admiration that he could only smile and laugh and surrender to the wild, sweet joy running through him.

And when even festival paused, there was Blathine.

ରଡ଼

On the Hill of Usna, only Coran the Druid and Conn of the Hundred Battles remained at the site of the ritual circle. A great storm had come up, sending banners of black cloud streaking across the sky, and the dancers had dispersed to gather their herds and find shelter for their horses. The storm had turned the entire sky green, and the more sensitive claimed the earth shook beneath their feet. They were all afraid, but at Conn's urging they had kept the dance going as long as they dared.

Yet the time came when even old Hundred Battles could not demand his people give more, and so they had been dismissed. Now just the chieftain and the druid waited together, watching the storm build. A great cold wind whistled around them, flecked with ice, out of its season. Along the distant horizon they thought they glimpsed flashes of fire.

"Never have I seen such a storm growing," Coran murmured.

The chieftain had become very cynical as a result of advanced age and the many sad events of his life. "You

don't suppose," he said, "that you've been misconduct-
ing the ritual? Could you be to blame for this?"

Coran recoiled. "I am not! Did I not bring you a vision
of your son? I could not do that and summon a dreadful
storm with the same ritual."

"Perhaps not." The old man shrugged. "But you must
admit we caught no glimpse of Fiery Hair this time."

"We did not. Yet I swear to you I felt him."

"Are you certain?"

"I am," Coran averred. "As we moved through the
steps of the dance it was as if I felt his presence among
us. The sensation was so strong I turned my head, expecting to see his face looking at me."

"Well? Did you?"

"Not his face . . . yet I saw something which never
was seen before on the Hill of Usna," the druid said. "I
saw a great wall of water rising, like a huge wave, and I
felt as if something very precious was in danger of being
carried away by that wave. I found myself reaching
out . . . and then the vision faded."

The old warrior's eyes were blurred as he responded,
"I had a similar experience. I thought it was my imagination. There seemed to be nothing around us but water
instead of air, and when I moved my feet it was as if I
were trying to dance in deep water. It took all my
strength to keep going.

"I told myself it was just because I am getting old," he
added ruefully.

"We are all old," said the druid. "Very old. The
youngest among us who still remembers Connla Fiery
Hair and cares about him has begun losing his teeth and
slumping his shoulders."

"What happens when we are dead?" Conn wanted to
know. "Who will there be to reach out to Connla then?
The bards may sing of him, but will that be enough?"

"We will tell his story over and over so that he is never forgotten," the druid assured his chieftain. "The children of your children's children will be taught to love the memory of your best and brightest son, and that love will always be a beacon calling to him, wherever he is."

Conn of the Hundred Battles sat down abruptly on the earth. "But I wanted to see him," he said. "I wanted to actually hold him in my arms again before I die."

The storm roared. And then, with shocking suddenness, it passed.

The sky grew lighter, the black streaks of cloud faded and became flags of silver as the sun reasserted its strength. The wind was no more than a whisper and birds began to sing again in distant trees.

The old druid looked around in surprise. "No storm? It seemed so certain, so terrible."

"Who can be sure of anything?" muttered Conn of the Hundred Battles, glaring at his own bent and arthritic knees and wondering if he would ever be able to stand up again. To dance again, in the ritual circle for his son.

Twelve

ON THE ISLES of the Blest, happiness had reached a fever pitch. Like every other emotion, human and fairy, joy had its peaks and valleys. The joy of the Sidhe was expressed in an outpouring excessive even for them, and Connla was its recipient.

Everyone seemed to want to do something for him. Blathine showered affection on him until he was finally reminded of one of the many lessons he had learned since coming away with her: One can have too much of a good thing, even air. Even pleasure. He found himself turning from Blathine as if she were a surfeit of honey.

And when he did, at once a jolly war was begun and sides were chosen and weapons pressed into Connla's hands. A fierce battle sprang up to offer a contrast to the joys of scented bowers. Connla fought and killed and laughed the hot, high laughter of a man at the height of his strength, and the warriors of the Sidhe clapped him on the back and praised his abilities. They were quite open in their admiration of him, quite fervent in their friendship.

Yet Connla could never quite forget he was not one of them. No matter how badly he was wounded, nor how he sought the sweet, brief sleep of oblivion, his brain never cooled in brief death and his memories stayed with him.

And no matter how often a feast was prepared, he was given only the magic apple to eat, though his mouth watered at the sight of the fairy food spread out to tempt him. "As soon as you are ready," Blathine told him. "You have only to say the word and you can eat to your fill; you have never tasted sweetmeats so delicious as these nor drunk wine so intoxicating. Take one bite and you will shed your human guise as easily as Finvarra lifted your weariness from you.

"Are you ready now, my Connla?"

Though he ached to say Yes, he did not. He looked with longing eyes at the food and shook his head. And Blathine, who was wise, did not push him further, but merely waited. She could afford to wait.

No time passed.

New delights were introduced to add merriment to the endless summer day. A herd of horses appeared, resembling the snowy animal with the proud high crest and long tail which had first carried Connla into enchantment. They were equipped with saddles of silver and bridles of gold, and caparisoned in silk. Connla was presented with the largest and most spirited of these horses for his own, and in company with many of the Sidhe he went for long gallops over rolling green hills.

On other occasions, the same horses were used as mounts for the fairy folk when they went hawking, for Finvarra brought a fine selection of magical hawks from his palace for the pleasuring of his people. These could capture any bird in the air with consummate grace. Fairy women were given smaller merlins to carry on their dainty wrists, though they pursued falconry with the same eagerness as their menfolk and cheered as lustily at a good strike.

And always there was dancing, and music, and a whole succession of games were set up and played on crystal tables beneath flowering trees. There was endless wagering, and no limit to the amount players might bet, for no one could be impoverished on the Isles of the Blest.

When the rules for these games were first explained to Connla he took part in them gladly, wagering huge sums. He would crouch over the playing board with a ferocious scowl on his face, moving carved pieces of alabaster and jade and lapis lazuli according to the prescribed patterns of the contest, concentrating on every move as if his life depended on it. When he won he was overjoyed; when he lost he was heartbroken.

But soon he realized it did not matter if he lost—he lost nothing of value that was not instantly replaced.

No one could be impoverished in the Isles of the Blest.

And when he won, he did not win anything he could not have had, anyway.

No one could be impoverished in the Isles of the Blest.

Blathine saw the discontent creeping across his face.

"You are remembering, and finding it painful," she said shrewdly.

"I am remembering that on the Hill of Usna we used to play a board game similar to these. Chess, we called it, and it was a very serious sport with us, for a man could lose all his cattle and find himself hungry at the end of the day."

"That can never happen to you here," she assured him.

"I know it. But it is a strange thing, Blathine—how the lack of peril diminishes the joy of winning."

"If you could forget, the games would seem fully satisfying to you," she promised him.

Her words were true, he knew it. In her lovely face he could see her concern for him and he understood she was willing him to accept complete and unalloyed happiness.

How easy it would be. How hungrily he longed to do so.

Yet a small voice at the very back of his head—or perhaps behind his head—spoke to him at the moments of greatest temptation. And though he could not always understand the words (for sometimes Blathine seemed to hear them too and would begin to talk to him very fast herself), he recognized the voice. The voice of the woman who had died in a wicker basket. The voice of a woman whose love for him had not died.

Love.

Connla kept remembering.

"If you love me, come with me now," Blathine had once said to him. He had proved his love by doing as she asked.

But did she love him? Could any of the Sidhe really love?

The question began to haunt him. Like a dragon stirring beneath the sea, it roiled his innermost thoughts and spread clouds of darkness over his happiness.

At last he knew he would have to ask her, though he did not want to; one part of him very much feared her answer.

He tried to reassure himself first by taking her into his arms and making a cold mental note of every effort she made to please him, weighting those efforts up like gold grains on a scale. Surely she must love me, he told himself, because she does this and this and this . . .

Only a fool would hesitate and question.

Only a fool, he told himself. Or a madman.

The thought frightened him.

In his father's kingdom young Connla had seen mad-men, people who were convinced of a different reality. They made strange remarks, odd gestures, talked to in-visible companions, rolled their eyes and shrank from horrors no one else could even see.

Am I mad? Connla thought.

Am I still, somehow, on the Hill of Usna, locked inside my own disordered skull?

Here was another question he dared not ask Blathine.

He summoned the one friend he thought might un-derstand, and little Whimsical came to him at once, as always, with a cheerful grin and a wink.

"I must talk with someone, Whim," Connla con-fided.

"I am all ears," said the other. Indeed, he almost was, for his pointed ears were the largest among all the Sidhe. With a happy sigh the little fellow settled himself com-fortably at Connla's elbow and prepared to listen.

"Do you know what madness is, Whimsical?"

A brief wrinkling of the brow, a shake of the head. "I do not know the word."

"Think," Connla urged. "You were human once. Do you not recall other humans who behaved in very strange ways for no reason? Some said they were mad and some said they were touched by the gods."

"Now that you describe the condition, I know what you mean, though I do not remember it myself. Madness. Ah, Connla, I heard a funny story about a madman once. It seemed that this . . ."

"Not now, Whim!" Connla said with uncharacteristic sternness to his friend. "Later you can tell me your joke and we will laugh together. But first, think about mad-ness and answer me truthfully when I ask you—could it be that I am mad?"

Whim drew back in astonishment. "It could not be at all! No one suffers from any affliction on the Isles of the Blest!"

"But suppose we are not actually on the Isles of the Blest," Connla persisted. "Suppose all of this, everything, is just something I am creating in my own head?"

"Me? You think you are creating me in your own head?" Whim was aggrieved. "What a terrible thing to say to a friend, Fiery Hair. To suggest that he does not even exist. I would not have thought you capable of such cruelty."

"Ah, Whim, I am not trying to be cruel. I am just trying to understand, to think clearly."

"Thinking! That is your trouble. You are still thinking, like a human person. If you would give all that up and be content to be happy and heedless you would be spared so much, Connla."

"I know. But there is always the possibility that I would just be giving in to madness, Whim. I need to *know*. Are you real? Am I actually here? Can you not help me?"

The little fairy man scratched his head, digging into his perpetually tousled hair with frantic fingers. "And how am I to answer you? How can I prove I am real?"

"Pinch yourself."

Whim started to obey, then stopped and laughed. "Pinching hurts and I left pain behind me long ago. I would not feel a pinch, so there's no proof."

Connla thought of Blathine. "If you feel no pain, do you feel pleasure?"

"I do indeed."

"How can you be certain?"

Whimsical stared at him. "I do not like this conversation, Connla. It makes me uncomfortable. I do not know what you want from me."

"Neither do I," Connla replied sadly.

To cheer him, Whimsical immediately launched into a windy and roundabout tale concerning three fish, a seven-headed bird with ruby eyes, and a stone that snored. Connla tried to listen, and tried to laugh even though the story, as always, did not seem funny to him. But his thoughts were elsewhere.

"Whim," he interrupted suddenly. "Do you never wish you could go back to being . . . what you were?"

Whim's mouth snapped shut like a turtle on a morsel of food. "Never," he said. Too quickly.

Connla's eyes lit with victory. "Aha! You *do*. Then you will help me."

The little man backed away from him. "I cannot."

"You can."

"I do not want to be hurt."

"I would never hurt you," Connla promised. "I love you."

"You do?" Whim's eyes were larger than ever and his ears quivered, from their round lobes to their pointed tops. "You . . . love . . . me?"

"Indeed I do, my friend. That is what friendship means."

"Oh, dear." Whim's chin wobbled. A suspicion of moisture glinted in the corners of his eyes.

"You remember love!" Connla exclaimed triumphantly. "You *remember*, Whim!"

The little fairy man held out his hands, palms upward, in a gesture of heartbreak and defeat. "I do," he said in a hoarse voice. "I did not want to. You should never have done this to me, Connla. You tore down a wall and let it all come flooding back in. Ah, woe is me!" He bent double and beat his small fists against his skull.

Connla was appalled at the result of his actions. He had just vowed never to hurt Whim, yet as soon as he brought back the memories of love, pain had come with them. Pain from the mortal world.

I *am* mad, he told himself. I must reject one world or the other forever; it is monstrous to try to stand with a foot in each.

He put his arms around Whimsical. "Forgive me, my dear friend," he pleaded. "I never meant . . ."

Whim waved him away. "It is all right, all right. I know you did not intend to make me suffer. I forgive you of course, Connla, for I . . . love . . . you too." His lips stumbled over the long unused word, but he got it out bravely.

They stood looking at each other like two mortal men.

"I will help you in any way I can," said Whimsical. Even as he spoke his ears seemed less pointed, his eyes less large.

"Then tell me, if you can. You are able to feel love. Can Blathine?"

Whim considered. "I doubt it. She has never been human; she was born to the Sidhe. But she makes you happy!" he added loyally.

"She makes me happy," Connla agreed. "It is myself who is making me unhappy. But I must resolve this, Whim, if I am ever to be content."

"What do you want to do?"

"I want to go back to the Hill of Usna. Just long enough to see those who love me, to assure myself they are all right. Long enough to see if there is anything there for me. One last look, that is all I really need. But I need that very much. Tell me: Is it possible?"

"It is. I think. The Sidhe travel back and forth quite easily. It would be a small matter to send you if they wanted to do so. But you have become very important to them. I do not know if they would willingly let you leave even for a heartbeat. Not until you have agreed to become one of them."

"As you did?"

"As I did. But what am I now that I remember again?" Whim asked in bewilderment. His eyes were still smaller, his ears had almost lost their points altogether.

"I cannot tell you," said Connla. "But I will take you with me. Whatever our fate, as fairy or mortal, we can share it together."

"I would like that," Whimsical replied with simple trust.

Instinct warned Connla not to go to Blathine with his request. She had worked so hard to bring him here, she would not be easily persuaded to let him have even one look back at the land he had left.

But Finvarra was another matter. The king of the Sidhe himself had said the fairy folk owed Connla a debt.

"Whim, do you know the way to Finvarra's palace?"

"I do indeed."

"Then guide me there," Connla requested. "I have a payment to collect."

With Whimsical at his side he crossed the verdant hills, the flower-starred meadows, the sparkling brooks of the land of the ever-living. Its beauties called out to him from every side, but he kept his determined gaze fixed straight ahead. At his side, Whimsical was quiet as the little fellow had never been quiet before.

"If you happen to catch sight of Blathine," Connla told him, "let me know at once. I would not want her to intercept us."

But Blathine did not appear. Connla wondered if she had already read his thoughts and knew his intentions. If so, would she attempt to stop him?

If not, did that mean she was not thinking about him all the time? Because she did not love him?

His poor skull ached with all its human thinking and questioning.

The spires and turrets of Finvarra's palace gleamed brightly in the distance. Connla began to walk fast so that Whimsical's shorter legs had to trot to keep up with him. When he noticed, he lifted the little man effortlessly onto his shoulder and carried him, with Whim's hands knotted into his fiery hair to hold himself steady.

Until he arrived at the palace gateway, Connla had forgotten about the maze of interior rooms. How would he ever find his way through them to Finvarra?

But Whim guided him effortlessly. "I have been in this land where no time passes much longer than you," the little man said. "I have often visited Finvarra's palace. Turn left here, then go up those stairs. No, right—no, left again. Down the passageway. Across the courtyard. Through the arches."

Following his passenger's directions, Connla soon arrived at the great audience chamber where he and Blathine had found Finvarra before. Once again the high seats loomed empty, and he paused before them, wondering where to look next.

Once again the king of the Sidhe materialized at his back.

"What is it you want of me, Fiery Hair?"

Connla whirled around. His eyes scanned the face of the magical monarch, searching for some sign of the warmth he had found there after his battle with the dragon. But Finvarra held his features impassive. Broad forehead, long and slender nose, a curved mouth above a narrow chin. Eyes abnormally large and brilliant, piercing in their gaze.

"You said you owed me a debt and I have come to collect," Connla announced.

"From me? And what can I give you that you do not already have?" Finvarra folded his arms, drawing himself up to his full height so he could look almost levelly into Connla's eyes.

Refusing to be intimidated, Connla replied, "I claim the one thing I do not have, the ability to travel beyond the Isles of the Blest and back to the realm of mortal men."

"So." Finvarra did not seem surprised. "So no matter what we do for you, you remain ungrateful."

"I am not ungrateful. I just want . . ."

"You want everything and no one has that," Finvarra told him, "—not even the Sidhe."

"One trip back to my birthland, is that too much to ask in return for what I have done?"

"You have the right to ask it," the king agreed. "But you must accept the consequences. Here, we are spared consequences, but in the realm of men they become a factor to consider. And you, Whim, what part do you take in this?"

Startled to hear himself so addressed, Whimsical twitched nervously atop Connla's shoulders. The little hands tightened in the bright red hair. "I am going with him," Whimsical replied in a slightly strangled voice.

"Are you now?"

"He loves me, I am his friend," Whim said defensively.

"Love. Mortals are obsessed with it," Finvarra sounded puzzled and contemptuous at once. "Is not Blathine's love enough for you, Connla?"

The young man stiffened. "Does she love me? Do the Sidhe love?" He had not been able to bring himself to ask Blathine that question, but he did not hesitate at this moment to ask it of the king.

Finvarra smiled a cryptic smile. "Put that question to her yourself." He raised one hand and drew a circle on the air. Within the circle there was a shimmer and a shiver. Then the circle enlarged to an oval stretching from the height of Connla's shoulder to the flower-carpeted floor—and Blathine stepped through, into the room.

"Ask her," Finvarra commanded.

Connla's voice seemed stuck halfway up his throat. He shaped the words with his lips but could not put enough air behind them to force them out. Watching him, Blathine twitched her lips with amusement. "Cowardice on the part of Connla of the Fiery Hair?"

"I am no coward," he answered hotly, relieved to find he could speak after all. "And I will ask you. Blathine, do you love me?"

The fairy woman cocked her head on her slender neck and gazed at him steadily. "I can work thirty-seven different kinds of magic," she said. "I can enchant and beguile. What more do you want of me?"

Connla moaned. "I want your love!"

Blathine turned toward Finvarra. "What am I to do?"

But the fairy king had no advice to offer.

Looking back to Connla, she said softly, "You ask for something which has no color or taste. You ask for a magic so powerful it cannot be caught in the petals of a rose, or sprinkled with the dust from stars. You were loved, Connla, on the Hill of Usna, but you walked away from it to be with me and accept what I offered, delights more easily obtained than love. You have known the Isles of the Blest; would you trade all they hold for the pain of mortal existence?"

"Yes . . . no! I do not know!" he cried in anguish. "I only know I must go back at least once, so I can weigh the two! I am held by the love of my people, and as long as that exists I cannot cut totally free of it and be with you completely, even if that is what I choose!"

"And is that what you choose?" she asked relentlessly.

He dropped his head. Whim ran a sympathetic hand over the shining hair.

"What say you, Blathine?" asked the king. "You brought him here; it is up to you to give him his answer."

"I will hold him, then!" she said with fire in her voice and sparks in her eyes; her opaque, obsidian eyes, blazing into Connla's.

"You do not love me," he whispered more to himself than to her.

Finvarra stirred. "But there is no pain on the Isles of the Blest, Blathine. I cannot let you give pain to this man to satisfy yourself."

"You said it was my choice!"

The king's smile was sorrowful. "I did not say 'choice.' I said it was up to you to give him his answer. We are the Sidhe; we have no choices."

It seemed to Connla's watchful eyes that Blathine's face grew subtly older. Her slender shoulders rounded, just a little, and looked more vulnerable. So vulnerable he longed to take her in his arms and tell her it was all a mistake, a game; he did not really intend to leave her even for an instant.

Be strong, my son, whispered that familiar voice at the back of his head. His mother's voice. *Be strong just a little longer. You are not hurting her; she cannot really be hurt. All the pain is felt by those you left behind on the Hill of Usna.*

With an effort Connla kept his hands at his sides and did not reach out to Blathine.

Finvarra said, in a grave voice, "The debts of the Sidhe are always paid. Just know this, Fiery Hair: the way we pay our debts does not always meet with the satisfaction of our creditors."

Turning, he strode across the hall, calling over his shoulder, "Come with me now if you would make your journey."

Blathine held out her round white arms to Connla. "Stay with me," she said in a voice like stars chiming.

"Whim?" Connla craned his neck so he could look up at his friend.

Whimsical shrugged. "Your choice, human," was all he said.

Connla hesitated a long, long moment, in which he was almost certain time did pass . . . then he broke into a run, following Finvarra.

As he passed beneath the arches he heard Blathine's voice call out to him, "Return to me. Do not forget!"

He ran out. A dreadful pain began burning in his breast.

Finvarra led the way from the palace, and no sooner were they outside than they found themselves on the beach. The same silver sand glinted with the same placid beauty; the waves rolled in gently, as if no dragon lurked beneath them. At the very edge of the water a boat made of crystal rode the shimmering surface of the water, tied with a golden chain to a piling of red wood.

"This boat will take you back to your birthland if that is your true desire," Finvarra said.

"Who will guide me? I am no ocean voyager."

"You still know so little about us," the king murmured. "The boat itself will guide you, of course. It knows the way. Both of you can entrust yourselves quite safely to it and be certain you will reach the shores of the mortal kingdom in due course, unharmed."

Connla looked longingly at the boat. It seemed very small for such an adventure, but it boasted a golden mast and a striped silken sail and there was an adventurous slant to its hull that tempted him. "How will we get back again?" he asked. "Will the boat return us just as easily to the Isles of the Blest?"

Finvarra chuckled without amusement. "Foolish human. I can never understand your kind. You want a guarantee; you make magic impossible.

"I will tell you this. I guarantee you will reach your first destination safely, but whether or not you can ever get back here even I cannot say. If you go, the risk is yours."

Connla hesitated. "And if I stay?"

The king's expression was unyielding. "If you stay, we will not ask you again to become one of us. We have a limited capacity to accept rejection. If you stay, you will retain all your memories and all your pains; all your human qualities, save only the ability to die."

"You have already lost much of what you might have had," Whim said. "And so have I!" he added. "But . . . oh, Connla, I think I remember the right way to tell a joke!"

"Save it," Connla advised him. "We may have need of something to make us laugh all too soon."

Finvarra stepped back. "You have made your decision."

"I have. Like the Sidhe, I find myself with no choice. I have already gone too far to turn back." He walked across the white sand, feeling it crunch softly under his feet, and stepped into the boat.

Finvarra followed him. At a clap of the king's hands fairy minions attired in spangles of seashells and seaweed ran forward and untied the golden rope from the pier. At once the crystal boat moved beneath Connla's feet like something alive, and began to nose its way outward to the open sea.

"Connla, wait! *Wait!*"

Blathine was running down the beach, waving her arms. Her hair had escaped its silver fillet and streamed behind her like a cloud of night. Her face was open and naked as Connla had never seen it before, and as the boat carried him ever more swiftly away from her he thought he saw love in that face.

Then he was too far out; her features were no longer distinct.

"Turn back!" he ordered the crystal boat.

It took no heed.

Helpless, Connla stood in the stern and held out his own yearning arms, reaching back toward the receding

island. He could see now that it was, indeed, an island—
a magical island with green woodlands and flowering
meadows and the spires of gleaming palaces rising into
a forever-summer sky. And on its beach the most beautiful of all women called and called to him, with longing
in her voice.

"What have I done, Whim?" Connla moaned.

"Just what I would have expected," his companion
replied, "if I had remembered sooner what it is like to be
a human being."

"I am sorry I got you into this."

"Do not be sorry for my sake, Connla. You did not
force me. I came of my own choice, so I suppose there
was something mortal left in me in spite of everything.
Even a spark that small would have made me discontent,
sooner or later. Perhaps I was never truly meant for the
Isles of the Blest."

"But you were happy there when I found you,"
Connla reminded him.

Whimsical clambered down from his shoulders and
took a seat in the prow of the boat. "I was not unhappy,"
he said. "Because I had forgotten unhappiness. But I am
not certain it is the same thing as being happy. The Sidhe
never worry themselves about such fine points." He let
out a tremendous sigh for such a small person. "When
we reach your homeland, do you suppose there will be
something to eat? All at once I feel a terrible gnawing in
my belly, like a great tooth chewing its way from back to
front."

At Whim's words Connla realized he was also hungry.
They must be moving out of the magical sphere already.

And the light was starting to fade. Night, which neither Connla nor Whimsical had seen for a very long time,
was creeping over the sea. They tilted their heads back
and looked up.

At the forgotten stars.

Thirteen

THE CRYSTAL BOAT raised its own sail on its own mast, adjusted its course, knifed smoothly through the water. Waves broke over the prow and sprayed the voyagers with mist, but the stability of their vessel never faltered. It made its way across the ocean at night as surely as an owl returning to its tree in the forest.

Connla felt inexpressibly weary. He slumped in the stern, one arm draped across the gunwale, and dozed. Each time he drifted off he shook himself awake again to examine the sensation of sleep; the almost forgotten sensation of sleep. How strange to sink into that cushioned formlessness!

"Whim, are you sleeping?"

"Uh . . . eh . . . I was. I think I was. Sleeping. Indeed, I was! How strange." Whim sat up and knuckled his eyes. "Where are we?"

The sea lacked signposts or landmarks. Connla gazed over an expanse of unrelieved gray-green. "We are heading toward the sunrise is all I know," he answered.

"Sunrise?"

"Look!" He extended an arm.

The sun came out of the sea to the east in a great flaring blaze of crimson and gold. Surrounding it, the sky was incandescent. The light hurt the eyes of the two men, making them blink. "Oh," gasped Whimsical. "I had forgotten how gorgeous it was!"

"So had I, Whim."

The smaller man winced. "Please do not call me that."

"I thought it was your name."

"I do not believe it is. I almost remember another name . . ." Whim paused, groping. "Not yet. But it will come back to me," he said with growing assurance.

The boat went on.

Time passed.

Rising ever higher into the sky, the sun cast a friendly warmth and then a fierce heat that was reflected off the water in an angry glare. Connla searched the crystal boat but found no supply of either food or drinking water. "I hope we make landfall soon," he said.

"I remember beer," Whim remarked in a dreamy voice. "And ale. And moist brown bread with a few unbaked kernels in it, crunching between my teeth."

"Be quiet, you are making me hungrier."

The other ignored him. "And roast meat and boiled meat. And kale. Remember how good and bitter and sweet kale is, with a lump of butter melting into it?"

"I will throw you out of this boat," Connla warned.

"And cheese. Now, that was lovely. I liked it very soft, not too old, with a little smell of goat about it." Whimsical sighed. "Black currants were good with that. My children used to eat black currants until the juice ran down their chins and stained them like purple beards."

"Your children!"

"Oh, I had children. And a woman. Such a plump, gentle woman." The small man's eyes glowed. "Before the sickness took them I had a lovely family."

"The sickness? Did they all die?"

"I believe they did; it is all coming back to me now. They died, and I cried out my hatred for the cruel fates that took them from me."

"And I have made you suffer anew," said Connla remorsefully.

The other man squinted at him through the glare. "But perhaps there is another plump and gentle woman in this land of yours, eh? Perhaps I might have more children, another family."

"If we stay. I do not know if I mean to stay." Connla thought of Blathine and felt his heart constrict; his breast still hurt with the pain of leaving her. "I am just coming back to see my loved ones once more."

"What if we cannot leave? What if the boat will not take us back? I do not know the way and I am certain you do not, either."

Connla had no answer but one. "If Blathine still wants me she will bring me back," he said.

"The Sidhe do not take kindly to rejection," the man who had been Whimsical reminded him.

A thin green line appeared along the horizon. The boat moved swiftly forward and the line lifted to become a wooded slope, with the inward curve of a basalt cliff below. As if it were guided by expert hands, the crystal boat glided into a narrow inlet which provided a perfect landing, and they felt the boat's bottom grate on solid shore.

The smaller man leaped out at once. "Which way?" he asked Connla.

Staring up at the cliffs, Connla tried to remember where such basalt was found. "East, I think," he said at last. "Quite a long way."

"Then we had best get started," said his companion at once. "Come on." He trotted off briskly in an easterly direction.

Connla looked back at the sea again, trying to envision the Isles of the Blest floating in the sunshine, just beyond the wall of human limitations. Sea birds were crying, far out, and he raised his arm to hail them. "Tell Blathine I am thinking of her!" he cried.

Then he turned to follow his friend inland.

The journey was long, for time no longer stood still. The sun rose and set and rose again, and the two men followed a hundred byways and trading roads and cart tracks and chariot ruts. Sometimes they were lost in impenetrable forests; at other times they had to skirt wide lakes. Connla took care to avoid being seen by the inhabitants of the occasional settlements they saw; this was unfriendly country, not within the sway of Hundred Battles.

To his surprise, his companion remembered skills of hunting and fishing far better than his own. In the twinkling of an eye the little man could make a hook out of a fragment of bone and catch them a tender salmon with ease, or bring down a wild pig with a javelin fashioned from a piece of flint and a tree limb. He was unerring in finding edible mushrooms and berries, and could run up a tree as easily as a squirrel in order to shake down a feast of nuts.

They did not go hungry, but celebrated the pleasures of human stomachs and appetites in a land where there was food in abundance.

"I had no idea this was such a rich country," Connla said with surprise. "Now that I think of it, even the Isles of the Blest could feed us no better than this."

"What you say is true," agreed the man who had been Whimsical, wiping a fine smear of grease from his chin as he finished a large meal of wild boar and badger meat.

"Viands there just have the spice of the strange and unusual, but nothing tasted any better than this." He belched and his nose wrinkled. "As good coming up as going down," he commented.

Connla laughed.

"Was that funny to you?"

"It was."

The little fellow nodded.

They resumed their journey, and soon the land began to look more familiar. "I recognize this plain," Connla said, "and that distant huddle of purple mountains, I know its shape, too. If we follow the curve of this valley toward the south and then back along the river beyond, we will come to the land of Hundred Battles."

Eagerness refreshed him. His strides grew longer and his short friend began to trot again to keep up.

When the Hill of Usna rose before them Connla felt his heart pounding. "I had forgotten how beautiful it is," he said softly. Yet it was like any other hill. Perhaps more sweetly rounded; perhaps greener. Not unique or special.

Merely . . . home.

A gentle twilight lent hues of violet to the shadows of the two men as they started up the well-worn path leading toward the fort of Conn of the Hundred Battles. Connla wanted to run, but he made himself adjust his pace to his friend's. It might be rude to seem too eager. But he could not help pointing out the beauty of the bellflowers blooming beside a stone wall, or the heavy hum of bees settling toward their hives ahead of the evening's chill.

Everything he saw seemed infused with a forgotten glamour, a magical luster composed of memories and nostalgia. Visions of the Isles of the Blest faded before the reality of his own homeland, his own familiar grasses and stones and pathways.

The carved gateway of the fort.

Beside the gate stood a guard in a saffron tunic, with a broad leather belt around his waist and a shortsword in his hand. A second guard, a few paces beyond, held a spear at the ready and met Connla's eyes with a hostile glare.

"What do you want here? Give us your name and tribe!"

The young man had never been challenged at this particular gate before. He checked his stride in surprise. "Do you not know me?"

"Should we?" asked the guard with a harsh laugh. "If we put your head on a pole atop the palisade we will learn to know you well enough before the crows eat your eyes out. Now again, tell us your name and tribe!"

He squared his shoulders and lifted his chin so the last rays of the dying sun could set his well-known hair ablaze. "I am called Fiery Hair; Connla, son of Hundred Battles."

The two guards looked at each other, then back at him. "That is impossible," said the one with the sword.

"I assure you it is not, and I demand to see my father."

"You say your sire is Conn of the Hundred Battles?"

"He is."

The two guards seemed uncertain what to do next. Drawing away for a short distance, they conferred in low tones, glancing at the strangers from time to time as they talked. At last the one with the sword advanced.

"Can you prove your claim?"

"I do not have to prove anything," answered Connla haughtily. "Send for my father; he will identify me."

"The gates are closed and barred for the night. We have orders to admit no one. There have been some skirmishes recently and our women are frightened. If you come back in full daylight, perhaps you will be admitted."

"I have come a great distance, all the way across the sea, to greet my father, and I am going to stay right here until I see him." Connla planted his feet and folded his arms across his chest. Standing just a little behind him, the man who had been Whimsical imitated his stance right down to the clenched jaw and outthrust underlip.

The guards spoke together a second time. "I have no orders," said the swordsman to Connla. "No matter what you say, I cannot let you in."

"Then I stand here for the night."

"Please yourself. I have no orders to prohibit you, either. But the night will be chilly and there are wolves in the forest. I suggest you gather some wood and build a fire for yourselves."

Connla took the suggestion. How long had it been, he wondered, since he had worried about the length of a night, or keeping himself warm?

When they had a good fire going his friend sat down cross-legged beside it and pulled his cloak more snugly around his shoulders. "You can stand there all night, Connla, but I am going to lie down." The little man yawned.

"Sleep, I will keep watch," promised Fiery Hair. Just in case word should somehow reach his father, and the old chieftain came to see if it was true, he wanted to be found on his feet as a warrior should be. A brave warrior who had fought a dragon beneath the sea and slain a monster formed of granite and won a hundred hard-fought battles on the Isles of the Blest.

The stars also kept watch, looking down on the Hill of Usna.

Now that he was caught in the flow of time, Connla realized how slowly it could move. No matter how often he threw his head back and looked, the stars had scarcely altered their courses or the moon moved more than a finger's width across the sky. The night threatened to become endless. He stamped his feet to keep them warm, he pinched his cheeks to keep himself awake. He tried calling out in his mind to his father, but even the dragon had been more receptive. He sensed no answering response; no response at all.

He might as well have shouted into empty sky.

Day, when it finally came, was gray and wet. Instead of dawn, there was a gradual paling into mist and an occasional harder spatter of raindrops. The air smelled of water. Connla's clothes were soon soaked through and he found himself shivering.

Beside the fire, which had sunk to a bed of coals, the man who had been Whimsical sat up. "Oooh, my every joint is stiff!" he complained. "Now I remember how much I hated sleeping on the ground." He got up creakily, rubbing his knees and shoulders in turn. "Give me a nice dry cave any time."

"As soon as my father learns we are here I will take you into a nice dry fort," Connla promised. "Our chieftain is well known for his hospitality. Even on the Isles of the Blest no stranger was ever made more welcome than he will make you, my dearest and most loyal friend."

The two guards of the night before had been changed, in the darkness, for two unfamiliar men. Once more, Connla explained who he was and demanded to see his father, and once more the guards jabbered away at each other while casting suspicious looks at him over their shoulders.

"Are you certain this is the right place?" his small friend asked dubiously.

"It is," Connla assured him. "We will see my father any moment now. Just watch the gateway . . . Ah! It opens!"

It did indeed open, and a chariot rolled out, drawn by a pair of bay horses with short, bristling black manes.

The charioteer was a red-faced and bony man, and beside him, arrayed in the many-colored cloak of a major warlord, rode a man Connla had never seen before.

"Where is Hundred Battles!" he called out in surprise.

The charioteer drew rein in. The chieftain beside him beckoned to one of the guards. "Who is this stranger?"

"He claims to be a man called Connla of the Fiery Hair," the guard replied.

The chieftain in the chariot laughed. "Preposterous! He has been gone for so many years hardly anyone even remembers him anymore." The man pointed an imperious finger at Connla. "Who are you in truth, and what do you want here?"

"I belong here," Connla said. "Just summon my father, I beg you. He will recognize me."

The man in the chariot gave a disgusted snort. "Madness. This one is a victim of madness, though the moon is not even full. And what about you, little fellow?" he said, turning to Connla's companion. "Who are you supposed to be?"

Drawing himself up to his full height, which was not very much, the little man who no longer had pointed ears replied, "I am called Gerrish the Cymbrian, and though I am short, I am supposed to be strong. Which I am," he added through clenched teeth, knotting his fists. "If you care to try me."

The chieftain narrowed his eyes. "I believe you, though you are a long way from your homeland. Why do you travel with this impostor?"

"Connla is no impostor but exactly who he says he is. I have known him . . . a very long time," Gerrish said, "and I do not understand why he is being insulted at his own stronghold."

"This is not his stronghold but mine," claimed the man in the chariot. "I am the son of Hundred Battles'

youngest daughter and I was fairly elected by my people
to be their leader."

"But what about Conn?" asked Connla, his face growing pale.

"Old Hundred Battles, tough as he was, could not live
forever. He died long ago. His sons did not live up to his
measure, and I took his place. The only one of his children who might have challenged me is the one they
called Connla Fiery Hair, but he ran away long before I
was born. You could not be he, stranger; he would be an
old graybeard by now and you have hardly any frost in
your hair."

Connla raised a hand to his head. "There is no gray in
my hair! I am young . . . Whim?"

"Gerrish," the other corrected, standing on tiptoe and
peering up. "I do see gray, though there was none before.
Tell me quickly, what about mine?"

"You are getting bald," Connla informed him. "On top."

Gerrish moaned. "Time is making its claims. We had
better try to go back. Though I did want to find another
plump and gentle woman and have some children on my
knee again," he added wistfully.

"I will not go back yet," Connla said, his face set in
hard lines. "I cannot believe what this man says. I know
my father still lives and I want to see him. I want to see
my friends and my brothers and the steward who was
always so good to me. I want to see . . ."

"Coran the druid," said a voice as whispery as dry
leaves rustling together.

Connla's head jerked around.

An incredibly old creature hobbled down the path
from the fort. Gnarled and twisted like a blackthorn
branch, swathed in layers of unbleached wool, dragging
himself forward in an act of sheer will, the man approached the little group around the chariot.

The guards fell back out of respect, knuckling their forelocks and keeping their eyes averted.

The chieftain in the chariot seemed equally impressed. "It is long and long since you came past the door of your own chamber, Coran. What possibly brings you on a journey of such difficulty for a man of your age?'

The ancient figure threw back its hood and turned a toothless face toward Connla. Trapped in the seams and fissures of that face the young man recognized, with a start, the mild eyes of his father's chief druid. They were all that remained of a once keen and foxlike countenance; all else was destroyed by time.

Coran was likewise peering hard at Connla. In his shred of a voice he said, "All those years we did the dance. All those years. At last even the most faithful lost faith, but we continued the dance out of habit. When Hundred Battles died I had thought we might stop, but by then it was so much a part of ritual that it went on after the reason was forgotten.

"And here you are, Connla." He shook his head in wonderment. "Here you are."

"This *is* Connla?" The chieftain hastily dismounted from his chariot and strode forward to take a close look for himself, though he had never laid eyes on the legendary Fiery Hair before.

"Indeed," the druid affirmed. "Now, perhaps, I can sleep and not have to wake up again. I had power after all. I have brought him home." The figure in the woolen cloak gave a sigh of weariness beyond all imagining and slowly sank to the earth.

They all bent over him, but Coran's spirit fled before anyone could touch him. Only an empty husk remained lying on the ground, muffled in fabric. Assured of the existence of magic, the druid himself had gone elsewhere.

The chieftain bowed his head. "So dies the very last of those who remembered you, Connla of the Fiery Hair. But I do not doubt his word. You are who you claim. If you wish, you are entitled to contest the chieftaincy with me. I suspect you might even be chosen by acclamation, all things considered."

The last of those who remembered you . . .

Connla pivoted slowly, looking up at the fort, out toward the land. A crowd was gathering now, a crowd of his father's people. Though they were not his father's people any longer.

Nor were they his, he thought. There was no familiar face among them. The only one he knew was Gerrish, who stood by his side smiling broadly at a plump young woman who approached carrying a leather water bucket.

"If you want to be chieftain here, I will stay with you, Connla," Gerrish said suddenly.

The man who was chieftain scowled. "There has to be a contest," he said. "I will not give way easily; it has never been said of Cormac mac Airt that he gave way easily. Do I not hold the kingship of all this land? Have I not been inaugurated at Tara itself?"

Connla was stunned. "Kingship of all the land?"

The other nodded. "Your sire, Conn of the Hundred Battles, engaged in a great war after you left him. He was seething with fury and fell upon Owen of the Southlands, and they fought for many seasons. At last they divided the entire country between them, and Hundred Battles was made ruler of the northern half, building himself a stronghold at Tara. I was on my way there now, in fact. It is not just for the Hill of Usna you must fight me, Fiery Hair—but for much of Erin."

"You must fight me," Cormac mac Airt had said. "Fight me for . . . Erin."

Fight and kill others and die yourself in a world where time is, where pain is.

Where life is.

Connla stood stricken, feeling his heart pound while they all stared at him, waiting to see what he would do.

Fourteen

THE LITTLE MAN who had now identified himself as Gerrish the Cymbrian shuffled his feet and cleared his throat. "I am no warrior, Connla," he said in a low voice. "I remember that most distinctly. I was a leather worker by trade and a storyteller by disposition, and I liked a hot fire and a good laugh. If you are going to go to battle, leave me out of it."

"I do not want to go to battle," Connla told him. "Not the way battles have to be fought here."

"But you must," Cormac mac Airt said in a hard voice. "The people will demand it and so do I. The issue of the kingship must be settled. And I warn you, Fiery Hair— no matter where you have been, or by what magic you have prolonged your life or increased your strength, I will fight you to the death."

Cormac mac Airt was tall and strong and proud, with a great mane of lustrous hair, and blue eyes that flashed like the sun on a summer sea. In his full manhood and power he was beautiful, and Connla had no wish to destroy beauty, even if he could.

He knew he could. He had not forgotten the magic arts that went with mastery of the blue sword.

The kingship of Erin, he thought. That was nothing I ever wanted or even imagined. It is not right that I must kill this fine man for it. But if I stay here, I will have to kill him.

And if I leave, if I find my way back to the Isles of the Blest, I will never again be cold enough to enjoy being warm, or sad enough to enjoy being happy, or dead enough to enjoy life.

"Aaagh!" he cried aloud, twisting his body with anguish.

Cormac mac Airt mistook the sound for a scream of challenge. There was a rasp as he withdrew his sword from its scabbard and in one long stride had it pressed to Connla's throat. "I accept," he said grimly. "Prepare yourself and assemble what support you will. If you have a champion to fight for you, my champion will meet him. If you do not have a champion, I will fight you myself and the winner will ask the people to name him as king if they find him worthy."

Gerrish, at the mention of a champion to fight for Connla, had taken several steps backward, until he found himself standing in the shadow of the plump woman with the water bucket. He smiled up at her; she smiled down at him.

Connla looked desperately around. There was no one to advise him; even the druid lay dead and safely out of it.

Then he heard the voice, the soft sigh on the wind.

At first he thought it might be Blathine's voice, for it was definitely female. But when he concentrated he recognized his mother's tones, less faint and faraway than they had been when she had spoken to him before.

So Cormac had not been entirely right. There was someone who still remembered him. She was dead too, his mother, but her love lived on and remembered.

I sought to save you, she whispered for his ears alone. *I sought to restore you to your own.*

"You have done," he replied, so low that no one else could hear.

Then I can go in peace, the voice said.

"But I am not at peace!" her son protested.

Ah, life is hard . . . came the answer, fading, fading.

The voice was gone.

Connla felt horribly alone.

He saw Gerrish looking at him. "I will not desert you," the little man called out. "I cannot fight for you, but I will not desert you. When you need me you can find me in the cottage of"—he looked up at the plump woman and she said something to him—"of the widow Derforgall."

So the man who had been Whimsical had no intention of returning to the Isles of the Blest, even if it were possible to do so. He had willingly stepped back into the river of time and would let it carry him. He had made a choice; a very human choice.

Connla felt Cormac's blade shift slightly beneath his chin. "Will you fight me?" the king asked.

Erin or the Isles of the Blest.

"I have never wanted to be a warrior," Connla replied. "Nor a king. If the people are happy with your leadership and prosperous under your guidance, I am content to leave things as they are."

Cormac's face darkened like the coming of a storm. "Are you saying you refuse to fight me? To give me the satisfaction of proving myself?"

"Why should I fight for something I do not want?"

"Because *I* want it!" roared Cormac mac Airt. "Enough of this talk. You are trying to confuse me by pretending you have no desire to take my place. But I am not easily confused, Fiery Hair. I have won many battles and planned many strategies, and no matter how clever you are, I am more clever.

"I do not believe you have come here all alone with just one balding dwarf for company. You have an army hidden somewhere. I can almost smell them. Your plan was to gain access to the fort of Usna and then, in the middle of the night, open the gates to your men and take it over. From this stronghold you could have attacked me. But I will not give you the chance; I am too shrewd for you!

"Send for your armies now, and I will send for mine. By first light tomorrow we will meet in this same place and either have a pitched battle or fight one-to-one, I care not which. Either way I will defeat you, Connla.

"And that is a promise."

He leaped back into the chariot, said a word to his driver, and the team of bay horses reared as the whip cracked over their backs. People scattered to get out of their way. The animals broke into a gallop and the chariot hurtled down the road and out of sight.

The crowd surged back to stare at Connla, to whisper about him, to reach out and touch him as the Sidhe had done when he first arrived on the Isles of the Blest. These people, too, reached out as if they wanted to steal a bit of his magic.

But he did not feel like a possesser of very much magic. He had even begun to wonder if he could, really, defeat Cormac mac Airt in battle. The man looked fit and formidable, and Connla was beginning to feel age seeping into his bones.

How long would he last among mortal men? How quickly would time reclaim him?

"'Balding dwarf' indeed!" someone sniffed at his elbow. Gerrish had come up to him, prickling all over with insult. "Perhaps I can learn to fight well enough to at least take a swing at that overpuffed warlord," he said to Connla. "We have until tomorrow—how quickly can you teach me?"

"There is not going to be a battle," Connla replied.

"No battle? But Cormac seems determined."

"Ssshhh. Come away." Connla plucked at his friend's cloak and led him a distance apart from the others, who did not follow them but continued to watch curiously.

"When the sun has set we will leave here, Gerrish. We will make our way, under cover of darkness, back towards the west. If we have good fortune we may get all the way to the beach where we left the crystal boat, and set sail for the Isles of the Blest."

Gerrish frowned. "What do you mean, 'we'? I thought you understood, I mean to stay here."

"Even if I leave?"

Gerrish considered his answer for a while, but then replied with certainty. "Travel is tiring and I am not as young as I used to be. If I go back to the Isles of the Blest it will just be the same thing over and over again. At least here, I can expect every day to be different and there will be surprises. I think that the one who calls herself Derforgall will be quite filled with surprises."

"You will die, you know. Probably very soon."

"And why not?" Gerrish asked with a shrug.

Connla could think of no answer. "I will bid you farewell now," he said. "And thank you for your friendship. You have been a grand companion to me as Whimsical and as Gerrish, and if a man has one such friend in a lifetime I think he is well served. I will remember you, whatever happens."

"Even in the Isles of the Blest?"

"Even in the Isles of the Blest. I do not know if they will take me into the Sidhe, now, and relieve me of memory. But I must try to reach them. I have no choice after all, Gerrish. I am still human, but even humans do not always have choices."

The little man was moved by the sadness in Connla's voice. "You could stay with us," he said. "I could ask Derforgall to hide you in her cottage."

"I have never been one to slink and hide and I will not begin now." Connla lifted his head. "I will at least go bravely, in whatever direction I go."

"Then I wish you well," said Gerrish. "And I will remember you."

Connla hesitated. "Perhaps it would be better for me if you did not."

The day passed, the sun rose and fell, many people came to see the miraculously returned Connla of the Fiery Hair. There was much talk on the Hill of Usna about the upcoming battle between Cormac and Connla. People began choosing sides and talking with excitement about weapons and chariots. The heat of contest ran through them like fire in dry grass, though many might die and many might weep afterward.

No one was left alive who actually remembered Connla, but there were many who had heard stories of him. Some of these brought him food and sat at his feet, begging him to tell them about his adventures.

He found their attention flattering but was reluctant to do as they asked. If he should describe the Isles of the Blest too glowingly, others might wish to go there. Might try to find ways to reach such a paradise, and have to pay a price they could not understand in advance.

But little by little they wheedled some of the story out of him, and once he had begun telling it he could not stop.

More listeners came, until a huge audience was gathered around him, drinking in his every word. Gerrish had long since gone off with Derforgall, mindful that he might have little time left and anxious to make the most of it. Connla sat on a tree stump and talked until his voice was hoarse and the sun sank low in the sky, and people listened and listened, their eyes full of dreams.

When the long twilight began they at last crept away to their own houses, their own snug fires and filled cauldrons, and left Connla of the Fiery Hair alone.

He spread out his coppery cloak and lay on it, looking up at the stars. The night was clear, but he knew this land. Between the batting of his eyelids clouds could scurry over the faces of the stars and rain could begin to fall. Yet he did not build a fire to keep himself warm, nor did he seek out any roof to shelter him.

This was his homeland, his birthplace. He might never see it again. He wanted to experience it as fully as possible, this one last time.

Time.

Time passed.

Connla did not sleep, but lay with his arms folded behind his head and his ears attuned to the sounds of the night. On the Isles of the Blest there was no night, so the small pipings of the evening insects were never heard, nor the faint music of nightbirds, nor the soft padding of night's predatory feet as agile killers stalked their prey through grass and woodland. Night had a different smell and a different sound from day, one that Connla had never appreciated before.

He tried to feel it all.

And then the first faint grayness showed in the eastern sky, soon to be replaced by a throb of rose light. Before that sunrise he must be on his way.

Connla was angry with himself for having waited so long. He got up as quietly as possible, shook out the folds of his cloak and wrapped it about himself. Walking on the balls of his feet he slipped away from his place outside the gate. The guards were dozing; they did not see him go.

He moved stealthily, keeping to the shadows, until he was beyond sight of the fort. And then he began to run.

Now he wished for the return of Fiachna's enchantment, and for feet that could fly like birds. Age was advancing steadily in his bones and he knew if someone saw him and sounded the alarm he could be caught, by even the slowest chariot.

He heard his feet thudding and his breath rasping in his throat. The two together seemed to make such noise he thought everyone must hear it. He pumped his arms and lifted his knees and ran as hard as he could. If someone saw him, he never knew. If an alarm was sounded, he never heard it.

When he could not run anymore, he fell panting into a swale of grass and lay there for a time, trying to get his breath back. Then he crawled on his belly to the edge of the grass and looked back the way he had come.

He saw no one following him. "Thank you for sheltering me," he said to the grasses.

But they made no answer. Yet, with the perceptions he had carried with him from the Isles of the Blest, he knew he was not alone and found that thought some small comfort.

When he had regained enough strength he went on.

Once more he avoided the scattered settlements he came across as he made his way west. The land was not empty; there were many farmsteads and smallholdings, and trading centers at crossroads, and every evidence of a prosperous way of life. The Erin that Connla sought to leave was surely as rich, in its own way, as the Isles of the Blest he hoped to reach.

I should never have left the first time, he told himself sadly.

But I did not know.

How could I know?

At last he came to the western shore and the dark cliffs he remembered so well from the day of his arrival. He approached them cautiously, almost afraid to look. He could not remember if, in his excitement, he and Whimsical—Gerrish—had moored the boat or not. Perhaps they had just left it bobbing on the tide, free to drift away.

I am not as brave as I thought I was, Connla said to himself.

But at last he went to the edge of the cliff and looked down.

There was no boat waiting at the water's edge.

He stood for a long time, just staring, as if he could make it appear if he wanted it badly enough. Sea birds called and the dark, sleek head of a seal rose above the surf, but there was no boat to be seen anywhere.

Connla slumped down and leaned his back against a rock. "I am to stay here after all, then," he said aloud, longing for the sound of a human voice.

He looked at the empty sea and the empty sky and felt empty himself. Where had all the magic gone? The shimmer, the sweetness, the unreal reality? Like youth, it had simply vanished, leaving an aging man behind, with no home and no destination.

"At least I can die," Connla said. "I have that. What was it my mother called it? Ah, indeed . . . the blessing of death. A way to throw off all memories, those that hurt and those that do not.

"Yet my mother came to me after she died, so she had not forgotten everything; she had not forgotten me. Is death as unpermanent here, then, as on the Isles of the Blest?"

Connla looked at the sea again, at the head of the seal coming in closer to land, and for a moment some trick of the light and his own eyes made the seal resemble a human. He thought he saw a face, a friendly smile, and automatically he raised one hand in a wave.

Then it was just a seal again.

Yet for an instant, there had been magic.

Magic in Erin.

"Is Erin really so different from the Isles of the Blest?" Connla wondered aloud.

He resumed staring out at the sea. He was waiting, just waiting, though he did not know what he waited for. To finish getting old and to die, perhaps. He looked down at his hands and saw the freckles on the backs of them. Soon those freckles would spread and become the spots an old man wore, the wide brown blotches of age. If he watched long enough he would see it happen.

But he did not want to see it happen. He looked up once more, westward again, across the sea . . .

. . . and saw something in the far distance. A tiny speck, it might be a trading vessel. Or another trick of the eyes.

As he watched, the speck grew larger. His heart was beating hard again, but for no reason. There was nothing unusual about the arrival of a trading vessel on the coast of Erin.

Connla got to one knee and shaded his eyes with his hand.

The dark speck became a recognizable shape. It was indeed a boat of some size, not large enough to carry traders and merchandise, however. A boat with a single mast and a—could it be?—a striped sail.

Connla of the Fiery Hair was on his feet. Through the sheer force of his eyes and his will he drew the boat toward him. Then all at once he flung himself at the edge of the cliff and began scrambling down its side, waving his arms, yelling, slipping and sliding and regaining his balance and plunging on down toward the beach.

Afterword

The Isles of the Blest is based on the ancient Irish tale of
Connla of the Fiery Hair, which, according to renowned
British folklorist Joseph Jacobs (1854-1916), was "the
earliest fairy tale of modern Europe." It contains an archaic account of one of the most characteristic Celtic
conceptions, that of an earthly paradise where heroes
fight and die gloriously and live again, and no one ever
grows old. This vision so impressed itself on the Euro-
pean imagination of the pre-Christian era that it ulti-
mately appears in the Arthurian cycles as The Vale of
Avalon.

But like any paradise, the Irish one has its price. The
Isles of the Blest are not easily entered nor easily left. The
man who would aspire to such a place must be prepared
to face many trials and give up more, eventually, than it
is mortally possible to surrender.

The hero of the story in the pagan version was
Connla; with the advent of Christianity in Ireland he
became known as Ossian and a new element was intro-

duced into the fable. The clash of the old and the new, of paganism and Christianity in the form of St. Patrick, became a feature of the earlier myth.

But without this morality play Connla's story still depicts a struggle in and for the human spirit, and is a spectacular example of man's earliest enchantment with the idea of an Otherworld.